# TALON

———————

## BOOK ONE

## BRENT TOWNS

**Talon**
Paperback Edition
© Copyright 2022 Brent Towns

Rough Edges Press
An Imprint of Wolfpack Publishing
5130 S. Fort Apache Rd. 215-380
Las Vegas, NV 89148

roughedgespress.com

Paperback ISBN 978-1-68549-047-8
LCCN 2021952836

# TALON

# CHAPTER ONE

---

*Brussels*

JACOB HAWK COULDN'T BELIEVE what he was hearing. "Say again?"

"Abort mission, Jake, I say again, abort mission."

Hawk set his jaw firm. "Negative, I'm going in."

The former SAS operator straightened his 6-foot-4 frame and reached behind his back to touch the handle of the Glock sitting there. The orange streetlamp above him showed his dark hair and unshaven face set in a grimace at hearing the voice of Archibald Thompson—operations manager of the MI6 team which had flown into Brussels the previous day—filling his head once more. "Damn it, Hawk, stand down. That's an order."

The thirty-year-old checked all around before starting across the narrow street towards the brothel owned by Lars Akker, one of Belgium's largest sex traffickers. "Hawk?" Thompson snapped again.

"Fuck you, come and get me. I'll be out front by the time you get here."

As he approached the red door of the terrace house in front of him, the guards stationed on both sides of the entrance stiffened and took a step forward. Hawk knew the package was in there, up the stairs, second door on the right. What he couldn't understand was the abrupt order cancelling the operation to rescue her.

The pair of overgrown apes dressed in tuxedos responded quickly, leaving their post and closing the distance between Hawk and themselves. As though synchronized, the guards reached under their coats, and Hawk was certain that their fists wouldn't come out empty. He pulled the Glock from behind his back and brought it around in a wide arc, striking the first of the guards up the side of his head. The man dropped to the pavement with an audible grunt. It was obvious to Hawk that the pair were not well trained, with the second guy faltering with surprise, the momentary lapse sufficient for Hawk to put him down beside his friend without a response.

Moving past the prone figures, Hawk stepped up to the entrance and pushed the door open, the unoiled hinges screeching a protest. Moving silently across the threshold, he went inside.

Within a few moments, the sound of gunfire could be heard.

———

THE RESULTING scene was reminiscent of an 80's action film. The first body lay supine on the carpeted floor of the foyer: a suited man armed with a handgun. The weapon lay beside his outstretched hand, his sightless eyes staring at the patterned ceiling. Crouched behind the reception counter, a young woman charged with greeting customers—attired only in a tight red leather corset and matching panties—cowering in fear at the violent events just witnessed.

Having managed to get a shot off, albeit a wide one,

the second man had been shot twice in the chest, and his body now lay sprawled on the stairs, the blood running out of him and pooling before making a viscous cascade towards the bottom.

At the landing, Hawk turned right, killing another of Akker's men before moving on and finding the door he required. He tried it. Locked.

As though the attempt on the door had triggered a booby trap, razor-sharp splinters shot out explosively from the door as bullets punched through it. Hawk immediately threw himself to one side, his right cheek stung by a thin sliver of wood.

The shooting stopped. He rose, lifted a size 12 boot to kick in the door, and walked inside. Facing him was a man desperately trying to reload his weapon. Hawk shot him too. As the latest body hit the dark carpet, Hawk moved quickly toward the crumpled bed where his target lay, her dress rucked up around her waist, revealing panties and a small tattoo. He began trying to bring her around.

"Molly, wake up. Come on, come back to me."

She moaned.

"That's it. Open your eyes."

Another moan.

Footsteps on the floor of the hallway warned him of approaching trouble. He turned and brought his Glock up to shoulder level. The shooter appeared, framed by the doorway. Hawk fired three times and the man fell back.

The slide locked and Hawk reloaded before returning his attention to Molly.

"Molly? Come on, girl, wake up, we've got to get out of here."

She'd been drugged, that much was obvious. Someone had dressed her in a short black dress which wouldn't have covered much even pulled down. Hawk checked her arms. He could see numerous tracks on them. More than likely heroin. "We're going to need Narcan, Alpha One. The bastards have drugged her to the point of overdose."

"Damn you, Hawk, you were told to abort."

"Just have it ready when I get out of here."

Hawk managed to get her up and then put her over his shoulder, walking quickly for the hallway and the landing at the top of the stairs.

One look told Hawk that way was no longer an option. Three armed men were running up the stairs. He raised the Glock and fired down at them. The first fell causing a domino effect, sending those behind him stumbling. The former SAS operator turned and hurried back down the hall. "Alpha One, change of plan. I'll be coming out the back."

No answer.

"Alpha One?"

Static.

"You bastard," Hawk hissed and moved faster despite his load.

He burst out the rear exit and clambered down the stairs into the alley which came in from the street behind. Once on the ground he looked around. "Alpha One, where the fuck are you?"

Still nothing. A shout from the top of the stairs made him turn. A man raised a weapon and fired in Hawk's direction, but Hawk was quicker, getting off an accurate shot. The bullet struck home, and the would-be killer fell forward, landing on the second step and sliding down the rest of the way.

With a grunt Hawk continued his passage trying to escape the clutches of Akker's hired guns.

"Hang in there, girl," he muttered out loud. "I'll get you out of this shit."

At the end of the alley, Hawk paused. He glanced left and right thinking maybe he would see the van, but there was no evidence of it anywhere.

He could hear them coming behind him. There was no way Akker would let him get away. The job was to rescue the girl and get her to the private airstrip where they would all board a plane for a quick hop over the border. Why there had been an abort given, he had no idea. But Hawk meant to find out. If they got out of Brussels alive.

"If you can hear me, Thompson, I'm going to fucking kill you when I get out of here.

————

THE TEAM WAS in the middle of packing up their crib, but the transmissions were still coming in loud and clear. Thompson turned to Davis, their comms specialist, and snapped, "Turn that damned thing off."

Davis swung around to look at his commander. "Tell me again why the hell we're aborting and leaving Hawk out there on his own?"

The team commander said, "Because he can't follow fucking orders. That's why."

"The mission was to get the girl. He's done that."

"The mission was aborted before then. Or are you hard of hearing too? There seems to be a bit of that going around."

"Sir, we've got hostiles closing in on Hawk's position," another specialist called over.

"Shut it down, blast your eyes!" Thompson looked around the room. "Can't you lot follow fucking *orders*?"

"Not when they're shit ones," Davis replied.

"It's not my call. This came down from the top. Like you and Hawk, my job is to follow orders."

They stared at him in stony silence.

Thompson shook his head. "Shit a bloody brick. Patch me through to him. And turn that van around. Shit, shit, shit!"

"Yes, sir."

Thompson grabbed his headset and put it back on. "Jake, are you there, over?"

———

HAWK HEARD the call crackle in his ear. "What? I'm a bit busy."

"The van is coming to get you. Where are you at?"

"I don't know, ping my bloody cell."

"What?"

"Just do it."

Thompson turned to Davis. "Ping his cell."

Davis did as requested, then turned to Thompson. "According to this he's about a kilometer away from where he should be, traveling at sixty."

Thompson's jaw dropped. "What? Hawk where the hell are you?"

Hawk's foot stomped on the brake of the stolen Audi as he put it into a tight right turn. Behind him a dark blue BMW did the same. Once it had negotiated the turn the passenger leaned out the window again, cutting loose with the MP7 they carried.

"Fucked if I know," Hawk growled. "Since you left me swinging in the wind I had to improvise. I carjacked an Audi S4. Right now, I'm blowing along a straight bit of street with some cocks in a BMW shooting at me. This all could have been avoided if you'd just done your fucking *job!*"

"We'll talk about that later."

More hammering from the rear of the Audi told Hawk that rounds were slamming into the fast-moving vehicle. Once again, he trod hard on the brake but this time he turned left.

Suddenly a set of headlights appeared in front of him.

With a loud curse he swung right into an alley barely wide enough for the Audi to fit down.

"I knew I should have stayed in bed this morning," he growled.

A moan from the back told him that Molly was still with him. But if he didn't get her the medication she needed, she'd die. "Alpha One, copy?"

The Audi smashed through a pile of trash which was almost hood high. The vehicle shuddered, slowed, then picked up its pace, a shower of sparks trailing behind it from the trash can trapped beneath it.

"Jake, copy?" It was Davis.

"I'm here, Harry."

"I've got you on ISR. You need to turn right when you get out of that alley, over."

"I need to get to a hospital—" Hawk braked as he shot clear of the alley, narrowly missing another vehicle. "Get me to a hospital, Harry."

"Are you hurt, Jake?"

"Negative; it's for the girl. They've all but OD'd her on heroin would be my guess. If I don't get her there, she'll die."

Thompson came on the air. "No go on the hospital, Jake. Bring her to us. We'll have our medic look her over."

"Do we have Narcan like I asked?" Hawk questioned as he swerved around a slow Jeep.

"Jake, turn left next street," Davis said hurriedly.

Hawk was about to say something when a Humvee appeared in front of him. A gunman standing in the turret with an automatic weapon. "Shit!"

Bullets peppered the side of the Audi as it slid into the turn. Hawk growled over his comms, "Where the fuck are all these vehicles coming from?"

"Jake, I count five all told converging on your position."

"How the hell do they know where I am?" Hawk snarled.

"Wait one, Jake."

"Don't take too long."

"Just keep going straight," Davis told him.

The Audi shot through an intersection with green-lit lights. The next however were red. Hawk glanced at the speedometer. It was sitting on sixty-five, and orange streetlamps flashed across the windshield like a disco ball. He glanced in the mirror and saw the bright headlights of two vehicles closing in.

"Hold onto your ass, Jake," Hawk muttered and depressed the gas pedal even further.

The Audi responded and the speedometer went to seventy. Hawk clenched his jaw as the speeding vehicle closed the distance between itself and the intersection, traveling like a missile on wheels.

Then from the left a black Mercedes appeared.

"Shit!"

Hawk swung to the left aiming for the vehicle's trunk hoping that it wouldn't stop. The Audi responded well to the sudden change of direction but when he jerked the wheel to the right it hit a puddle and the rear kicked out forcing him to correct the slide.

Grinding his teeth together, Hawk bit back a curse as he waited for the bone-jarring crunch of the rear wheel hitting the curb. However, the Audi's traction control kicked in and helped the situation.

Hawk looked once more into the rearview mirror and saw the lead chase vehicle slam into the Mercedes just behind the rear passenger door. The back of the car seemed to disintegrate on impact, debris spraying through the air.

The chasing vehicle veered violently to the left and crashed into a parked car where it burst into flames.

Hawk said, "Davis, I need to know what you've got planned."

"OK, Jake, we've got ourselves a situation. I'm picking up a low frequency transmission coming from your vehicle."

"What do you mean, low frequency?"

"Like a tracker of some kind."

"Where the hell would—bugger me. They've put a tracker in her."

"That would be my guess."

"Can you disable it?" Hawk asked.

"No, not from here," Davis replied. "That's not all. You've now got seven vehicles closing on your position."

"Christ. Tell me where to go."

"It doesn't matter, Jake, they'll still find you."

"What are you saying, Davis?" Hawk asked knowing what the answer was going to be.

"You need to leave her, Jake."

"No way. Come up with something else."

"There is nothing else, Jake." It was Thompson this time.

"Then get working on something. I'm not leaving her. You can shitcan that idea for a bag of monkeys right now."

"Jake—"

"Fuck off. Davis, find me a way through."

"I'll do my best, Jake. But there could be more out there that we don't know about."

"Just tell me where to go, I'll do the rest."

"All right, I'll try to guide you to the RV. We've got a helo inbound with some shooters on it. If you can make it, you might be alright."

Beside Davis, Thompson muttered, "Great, we'll start a war on foreign soil."

"Do it," Hawk snapped.

"Turn left—now!"

Hawk braked heavily, went down a couple of gears

and booted the gas pedal. The rear wheels spun then bit. The Audi once more shot forward pushing Hawk back into the seat. Tires squealed in protest, leaving traces of rubber on the street.

"Two-hundred meters ahead there's a hard right. You need to take it. But watch out it's a one-way street and you'll be going the wrong way."

"Roger that."

"You're coming up on it in three...two...one...abort! Abort!"

Hawk corrected from the anticipated turn just as a police vehicle shot out of the one-way street. Lights were flashing and siren blaring. It slid sideways, headlights bouncing like they were on pieces of elastic. It straightened just in time for the remaining chase car to slam into it from behind.

The vehicle launched into the air, doing the obligatory 8o's action movie turn in midair before crashing down on its roof. "That'll do it," Hawk grunted. Then, "Talk to me, Davis."

"It looks like the local coppers have joined the party, Jake. Makes things a little more interesting."

"You don't say."

"Turn right!"

Hawk swung hard on the wheel and the Audi took the turn sideways. "I feel like I'm going in circles, Davis. This isn't good."

"I'm doing my best, Jake. Take the next—fuck, you went past it."

"Calm down and let's get this right. Try again."

"Turn left."

Hawk took the corner and floored the gas pedal.

"You've got three kilometers on this street before the next turn. The only problem is, there are six vehicles closing in on you and there's a narrow bridge about one klick up. It's going to be touch and go, Jake."

"Hold my beer, Davis," Hawk said as he gave the Audi more gas.

"What?"

"I heard it once from an Aussie I was on deployment with, in the desert. He—"

"You know what, forget it. How's your passenger?"

Hawk suddenly realized that he hadn't heard her for a while. He maneuvered the rearview mirror so he could look in the back seat. Molly was still laying down but through the flashes of the orange street lamps he could see the discoloration around her mouth.

"Shit, shit, shit. Davis, we've got a big problem. I think she's stopped breathing."

A drawn-out silence reached out to Hawk over his comms. "Davis, talk to me."

"You're still ten minutes out from the RV, Jake."

"She doesn't have ten fucking minutes."

"Sorry, Jake, I don't know what you want me to do."

"Where is the van?"

"Too far out."

Hawk slammed the wheel with the palm of his hand, opened his mouth to curse, when—

"*Jake!*"

WHAM!

The Humvee hit the Audi from the side. Its front buried itself into the rear quarter panel, kicking the Audi around into a violent spin. It whirled across the street and cannoned into a parked vehicle. Inside, Hawk was slammed from pillar to post.

The Audi kicked back around and then flipped, rolling several times before coming to a halt upside down.

———

"WHAT HAPPENED?" Thompson demanded.

"Jake, can you hear me, over?" Davis said, ignoring the question.

"What happened?" Thompson tried again.

"Jake, talk to me."

"How about someone talk to me," the MI6 man said.

"He got hit," Davis replied. "There was an X-Ray I didn't see."

"How could you not see it?"

Davis glared at his boss. "Maybe because we're fucking half packed up."

"All right, all right, where is the van?"

"Still a couple of minutes out."

"Get it there as quick as you can. In the meantime, keep trying him."

———

"CAN YOU HEAR ME, JAKE, OVER?"

Hawk coughed and then groaned. His body hurt and he could smell gas. "What hit me?" he moaned.

"Thank God," Davis replied. "Are you alright?"

"I don't know. What happened?"

"You got hit."

"By a freight train by the feel of it."

Hawk's head seemed to be filled with cobwebs, everything was fuzzy from the high impact of the crash. Then he remembered Molly, and everything started to clear. He tried to move and look in the rear of the overturned Audi. He gasped as pain shot through his left shoulder. He grabbed at it, feeling the bulge at the top. His shoulder was dislocated. No wonder it hurt.

Ignoring the pain he twisted further, glass cutting into exposed skin. When he was far enough around, the light from one of the streetlamps showed him just enough to see that the girl wasn't there.

"Oh, no. No, no, no."

He wriggled urgently to get himself through the opening where the window had been. Dragging himself with his right hand, Hawk felt more glass bite deep into his flesh.

Blood ran through his whiskers and dripped from his chin, the cut at his temple feeding the flow. Other pains started to emerge now as the adrenaline began wearing off. Ribs, leg, head all added to the pain radiating from Hawk's shoulder.

Once clear of the Audi, he staggered to his feet, more out of sheer determination and willpower. He glanced around frantically, taking in two men walking towards him. He blinked away the fog, frowned, and noticed the weapons they were carrying.

Hawk grabbed for his Glock and was relieved to find it where he'd put it. It came out too slowly, like cold molasses from a jar. By the time he had it raised, the two men had already opened fire.

Bullets cut through the air close to Hawk as he tried to steady his gun hand. He squeezed off a shot and saw the first shooter whip around with a bullet to the shoulder. Hawk grimaced as he shifted his aim and fired again.

The second shooter went down with a round in his stomach. Both men remained a very real threat. Hawk limped forward, blood flowing from the gash on his right thigh. He reached the two squirming figures and shot them both, ceasing any further movement. Hawk looked around once more for Molly.

He gasped when he saw her. She lay in the middle of the street twenty meters from where he stood. Her limp form twisted in an unnatural manner. "Oh, shit a brick."

Hawk limped towards her prone form praying that he would find some sign of life. The sound of screeching tires caused him to turn. Urgent shouts drew his attention to the three men climbing from the dark SUV. "Bloody hell."

The Glock came up once more as muscle memory

took over. The weapon crashed twice, and the first shooter collapsed. Hawk advanced towards them, his legs moving in an awkward gait. Hawk's teeth ground together as red hot anger began coursing through his veins. The Glock bucked in his hand and the second shooter went down.

The third shooter fired and a round clipped Hawk's bad left arm. He stifled a cry and sank to his knees. Twice more the handgun roared, and the third shooter went down with a round in his throat. The man clutched at the ghastly wound trying to stem the blood flow but it was a futile gesture. His ministrations weakened as he died within moments.

Once again Hawk struggled to his feet. "Davis," he grunted. "Where's that fucking van?"

"It'll be onsite directly. Thompson wants an update."

The former SAS man dropped beside the girl. Her eyes were wide, mouth slack. "She's dead," Hawk replied bitterly. "Tell the prick she's frigging dead. I hope he's happy."

"Jake, you've got two more vehicles inbound."

Hawk dropped out the almost empty magazine from the Glock and replaced it with a fresh one. Then he dragged himself wearily to his feet and said, "Let them come."

———

WHEN THE VAN ARRIVED, Hawk was down and bleeding. The three men inside poured out through the side door, each armed with SA8os. They picked targets as they emerged and dropped threats at will. With practiced ease they moved towards their fallen comrade and set up a two-man perimeter while the third leaned over Hawk. "He's still alive. I don't know how; he's got four bullet holes in him.

"Get him in the van, we'll triage him there."

"What about the girl?"

Bullets were still incoming, snapping close.

"Leave her, she's got a tracker on her."

"But—"

"Orders."

The man who'd been leaning over Hawk grabbed him by his collar and started dragging him towards the van. The motor was still running, the driver behind the wheel. "Hurry up, get him in."

The remaining two shooters made a fighting withdrawal back to the van, covering their comrade. They climbed inside and slammed the door shut. "Go, go," one of them shouted at the driver.

The van sped away into the darkness.

In the cargo hold, Hawk's eyes fluttered open. He stared up at the man leaning over him who worked to save his life. He gave him a weak, bloody-toothed smile and said, "What took you so long, Ginger?"

"Stopped at the store to get some smokes," the man called Ginger replied.

Hawk gave him another weak smile before stiffening and his eyes rolled back in his head. "Shit a fucking brick," Ginger growled as he thumped on Hawk's chest. "Don't you die on me, Jake. You do and I'm going to be frigging pissed, mate. Don't you die."

# CHAPTER TWO

---

*Berlin, 1 Year Later*

ANJA MEYER STARED at the large screen before her. She counted six dots; each dot represented one of her operatives. A larger one was the emergency response team which would assault the target when it was needed. Twelve men specially trained for their mission.

The German version of Hermione Norris adjusted her headset atop her short blonde hair. She brought the headset mic closer to her lips. She whipped her hands down the lower half of the jacket of her pantsuit and said, "What have we got?"

The Federal Intelligence Service operations room became instantly alert as they waited their turn to speak.

Operation Valkyrie had been in motion for the past month. Ever since they'd received word of a terrorist operation possibly forming inside their borders. There were supposed to be two cells. The one they were about to take down and another they were having trouble locating. So, the decision had been made to take down the first in the hope it would stall the second, which would give them time to find it.

"All agents are in position, Miss Meyer," came the first voice to reply.

"Good. Do they have eyes on the target building?"

"Yes. They report that all is quiet."

"Lights?"

"Yes."

"Are we ready to cut the power?"

Another voice answered. Female. "Yes, Miss Meyer. I'm on the line with them now. When we give them the word the whole block will be blacked out."

Anja nodded. "Make sure they respond promptly, Ilse."

"Yes, Miss Meyer."

"Karl, is the breach team ready?"

"Yes, Miss Meyer," a third voice replied.

As she double and triple checked everything, a pattern began to emerge. Anja Meyer expected nothing but the best from her people. And in return they expected the same from her.

She'd been in command of the special operations branch of the intelligence service for two years. In that time, the thirty-four-year-old Stuttgart native had excelled in her position. Working and coordinating with intelligence agencies across the world, her role had been pivotal in joint taskforce operations in North Africa, the Middle East, Afghanistan, Europe, and Russia. To her bosses, Anja and her team became the go to people for the tough jobs. This one, however, was different. On home soil, if things went wrong, no matter the skill sets of the team, heads would roll.

Anja stared at the screen in front of her. "Bring up bodycams on the assault team."

Beside the main large screen, a second one came to life and split into many panels as the cameras came online. At the top of each box was the data on the operator and their vitals.

With a nod of satisfaction she said, "All right. Bring up the UAV footage."

A third large screen lit up showing footage from the circling unmanned aerial vehicle. Although it was dark, the vehicles on the street outside the unit block could still be distinguished beneath the streetlamps.

Anja took a deep breath and closed her eyes visualizing the details as proposed for the progress of the operation. Satisfied that all was in order for the mission to proceed, she opened her eyes and slowly let the air out of her lungs. "Ilse, cut the power. Have the assault team move in. Let's do it."

The team gelled and commenced moving like the well-oiled machine that it was. Every decision was made as the mission progressed, according to occurrences. Anja was apprised of each through her headset, however, she only spoke or intervened if she thought it was crucial. Otherwise, she let them do their thing.

Instantly on the screen Anja saw the power go out then she heard Ilse's voice, "Power is down."

"Assault team moving in. ETA one minute." That was Karl.

"Do we have any reaction from the building?"

"No, Miss Meyer."

"Let's hope it stays that way." She frowned. "Have our assets move in closer to seal off any escape routes."

The dots never moved.

"What's going on, Felix?" Anja asked, impatience evident in her voice.

"I'm trying to get them online, Miss Meyer," Felix replied.

"What do you mean, trying?"

"Our comms are screwed or something. I can't raise them."

"Couldn't you get them before?"

"Yes, Miss Meyer."

"Then get them back."

"Breachers moving into position."

Anja looked at the screens, her eyes flicking left to right and then back again. "What's that?"

"Where?"

"Near the point where Rolf is," she replied.

The picture zoomed until it could go no more. "Make it clearer."

"Alpha Team ready to breach."

Anja ignored the radio chatter as she tried to discern what it was that she was seeing. Then her eyes widened when she realized what it was. A body. Someone had killed one of her people.

"Breachers are in the building."

"No!" Anja snapped. "Abort, abort now!"

"All teams abort. All teams abort."

"What's going on?" Karl asked.

"Rolf is down. I need to know—"

BOOM!

The sound echoed through the room and the body-cams' screen went blank, the only screen that remained glowing was the one showing vitals. Anja froze and looked on with horror at the third screen. "Is that an explosion?"

"Wait one, Miss Meyer."

Anja glanced at the vitals of her Alpha team. Every single one was flatlined. "What's wrong with the signal from the Alpha team, Karl?"

"They're not there."

"What?"

"They're not there, Anja, they're gone."

Protocol was hurriedly going out the window. "They can't be gone."

"Confirming an explosion onsite," a new voice joined.

"Was the Alpha team inside the building?"

"Possibly," Karl said.

"Were they?" Anja demanded.

"Yes, yes, they were. The Alpha team is down."

"Shit," Anja exploded, the first real sign of a crack in her normally cool exterior. "Get them some help. Deploy Bravo Team to the site. Secure everything. Reach out to the *Bundespolizei*. Tell them we need their help. The whole scene has to be secured for five blocks in every direction. Understood?"

Her team swung into action doing their best to follow her instructions. Anja stared at the screens. Something had gone wrong, and she meant to find out what it was.

"Miss Meyer?"

Anja turned to see a thin-faced woman standing there with a confused expression on her face. "What is it?"

"A bomb has just gone off—"

"Yes, I know that," Anja said abruptly. "I just saw the blasted thing go off."

The woman shook her head. "No. This one went off in the center of Berlin."

Anja's face paled. "How could she and her team have got it so wrong?

———

*Berlin, 2 Months later*

The investigation and inquiry were conducted with the utmost efficacy to satisfy the public and to protect the politicians. Anja's interrogation—for that's what it was— had lasted for two solid days by every member of the committee. From the outset it was clear they needed a scapegoat—someone to blame. The head of the intelligence service had ultimately distanced himself from Anja who was left hanging out to dry.

It wasn't enough that she'd lost her team on the ground during the operation. Now they wanted her career as well. The loss of two hundred lives would do that.

In the aftermath of the explosions, Anja learned that the terror cell hadn't been Middle Eastern as she'd thought; a cell wasn't responsible at all. It was a Russian, an arms dealer and sex trafficker named Viktor Medvedev. After Anja and her team had broken up a deal worth fifty million dollars the previous year, Medvedev had immediately began plotting his revenge resulting in what Anja had called Valkyrie and the failure that it became.

Now face to face with Wolfgang Berger, her immediate superior, his façade was an expression of grim futility. His words were somber as he said, "The report will be released to the public tomorrow, Anja. I have a copy if you wish to read it."

She shook her head. "I already know the outcome," she said bitterly. "It will exonerate anyone above me, with the blame laid squarely at my feet and those of my dead team. As we know, anyone in the higher command structure was quick to flee from the scene like scared rabbits."

He looked at her gravely before saying, "It would be better if you resigned immediately."

"Why?"

Berger stared at her. "It would be better for the service—"

"Better for you and those above you, don't you mean? Yes, this was my operation but everyone in the command structure saw my report and ticked it off."

"The public won't see it that way. The command structure will make sure of it."

"Of course, they will," she snorted. "How many times has my team saved this country from a devastating attack? How many, Wolfgang?" Anja had shown quiet restraint until then, but now they were forcing her out, she had no intention of going quietly. "More times than you care to admit, isn't that right? But the very first time one gets through, it's more convenient to throw us to the wolves so that you all save losing face!"

"It is what it is."

"Well, it's fucking bullshit," Anja hissed, losing the last of her control. "So, what now? Am I to be pushed into another department or cast out in the cold?"

Berger remained silent.

Anja nodded. "I see."

Her boss held out his hands in a helpless gesture.

Anja said, "You know, the media will be clamoring for satisfactory answers to all their questions. They won't be so easily appeased."

Berger's eyes narrowed. "Are you trying to blackmail me, Anja? Because if you are, it won't work."

She shook her head. "I have no desire to blackmail anyone, merely advising you that the media will be all over this once the report comes out with my name at the top of the list."

"If you say anything that may be construed as—"

Anja had heard enough. She rose from her chair, tossed her credentials onto the desk in front of her and said politely, "Fuck off."

Then she turned and left the room. Her illustrious career in the Federal Intelligence Service was now over.

———

*Richmond, Virginia, United States*

Dark-haired, twenty-one-year-old Jimmy Garcia took another pull at his twelfth Red Bull can and let his fingers dance across the keyboard. He was on such a high that all sense of time had been lost six hours into this ten-hour stint. His eyes were fixated on the computer screen as he watched every response made by the computer tech on the other end.

"Who said the FBI had all the good techs," he crowed

as he blocked another attempt to backdoor his system. "Have to do better than that, asshole. BAM!"

No sooner had one attack been stopped than another began. Jimmy had to admit, whoever it was on the other end, be it guy, girl or otherwise, was good but not on par with him.

It had started out as a buzz hack. Just something to do to prove he could still do it. Not intended to be anything sinister, but some harmless computer fun. But getting in had been so easy, Jimmy was disappointed at the lack of a challenge. So he'd tripped one of their warning systems to see what would happen. And it had gone from there.

At first, he just toyed with the person on the other end. Then they showed some promise, and his ego got the better of him. Everything went downhill from there.

Inside his dimmed living room were wall-to-wall systems providing him with all the power required by Tormenter6743.

"Come on, come on," Jimmy coaxed as he typed in more code to block the latest attack. "Jimmy has got your number."

His smile dropped instantly when his screen changed and the words, Knock, Knock! appeared.

Suddenly the front door flew wide with a loud crash. "FBI, FBI!"

"Holy shit!" Jimmy exclaimed and just about fell out of his chair.

Armed men rushed into the living room with guns pointed at him. "Get on the floor! Get down, now!"

"What are you doing? Hey, what is this?"

One of the FBI team holstered his weapon and forced Jimmy to the floor. "You're under arrest, punk."

"What for? What did I do?"

"Save it."

"You've got the wrong guy."

The officer rolled him onto his back and a female

agent dressed in a pants suit stepped forward and looked down at him. "Jimmy Garcia, you're in a lot of trouble."

"Oh shit."

———

*Sierra Leone*

John "Grizz" Harvey was a big man. Six-five in his socks, he was broad of chest and shoulders, and had a single tattooed sleeve on his left arm. The hair he lacked on his shaved head was made up for on his face by a bushy black beard. Not the kind of man you wanted to meet coming at you in a dark alley. But the kind of man you wanted leading you when shit got real, and you were down in the dirt slugging it out with bad guys with guns.

And right at that point in time, the four-man team of shooters were up to their necks in jungle, mud, and crazy drugged-up assholes trying to kill them.

"Frag out!" Harvey called, throwing the fragmentation grenade at a group of militia soldiers coming towards him. He dropped to the damp earth and waited for the explosion.

It came with the accompanying screams brought on as razor-sharp splinters tore into and mutilated soft flesh.

In the wake of the blast, the big man came up to his knee and commenced issuing rounds from his suppressed Heckler & Koch 416. The fire selector was set to semi and each time his sights settled on a target, the big man fired twice. Once was dead, twice to be sure.

"Changing!" Harvey dropped out a spent magazine and replaced it with a fresh one. He glanced at the thick-set, dark-haired man beside him and said over the cacophony of battlefield noise, "Linc, take Nemo and fall back. Set up a base of fire. I'll be right behind you."

"Roger that," the operator called back. Then, "Moving."

Harvey kept up his rate of fire as the militiamen kept coming out of the jungle like crazed animals, with no regard for their own safety, but with the intention of killing the intruders. The big operator had seen nothing like it except in zombie movies. Whatever they were on, it certainly fucked them up.

Over on their right flank he could hear MacBride cutting loose with his M249. "Mac, fall back to Linc. Set up the claymores."

"Roger, boss."

Harvey kept up his rate of fire before he, too, made to fall back to the others.

The firefight had been going on for the past twenty minutes. The team had been inserted into Sierra Leone to collect a package that had fallen into the hands of a local war lord. What Cross Swords—the company they worked for—failed to tell them was that the package included two hundred million dollars' worth of Blood Diamonds.

A princely sum that the war lord had no desire to lose, so was throwing everything he had—including a whole army—at them, without regard for any losses inflicted upon same.

"Delta One, this is Eagle One, copy?" Harvey said into his comms as he moved through the thick undergrowth.

"Roger, Eagle One, we read you loud and clear, over."

"We're in heavy contact and falling back toward the primary LZ, over."

"Roger, Eagle One. We have you on ISR. Be advised that the enemy is trying to flank you on the right."

"Roger that. Break. Mac, forget my last transmission. Meet me on the right, they're trying to get around us."

"Copy."

Harvey changed his angle of retreat and moved

further right until he'd traveled around fifty meters. "Delta One, Eagle One. Sitrep. I can't see shit."

"Roger, Eagle One. You've got ten or so hostiles thirty meters out and closing fast. Get ready."

The crash of undergrowth behind Harvey made him look around. A solidly built man with a bandana wrapped around his head appeared cradling a light machine gun. Harvey grunted. "Get ready, they're coming in hot."

Almost instantly the green undergrowth below the triple canopy above them parted and the first handful of militiamen rushed forward. Both operators opened fire with their weapons and the attackers jerked a macabre death dance under multiple bullet strikes.

AK-47 rounds hammered out from within the green wall and dug into the soft earth around Harvey and MacBride. The big team leader grabbed another grenade from his webbing and pulled the pin. "Frag out!"

He threw it hard, watching it disappear into the jungle ahead of them. Within seconds an explosion rocked the area. "That ought to slow the suckers down," Harvey growled.

They pulled back towards the rest of the team, but as they drew closer, the firing grew in intensity. "Linc, sitrep?"

"We can't hold out much longer, Grizz. We need to pull back."

"Clack off those claymores and get the fuck out. RV at the creek we crossed coming in."

"Roger that."

The jungle came alive. CRUMP, CRUMP, CRUMP! Three claymores ripped the undergrowth apart. Harvey turned to MacBride. "Come on. Move."

They started to run through the jungle, bounding over fallen trees, and dodging the ones still standing. They crashed through the undergrowth until they reached the creek. It was a narrow strip of slow-moving water which offered itself as a natural defensive position.

Harvey and MacBride waded across and took up positions behind a couple of rocks. Not far behind them were the other two team members. No sooner had they taken cover when their pursuers appeared on the bank of the stream. The M249 came online almost instantly. MacBride depressed the trigger and the weapon spat death. The first five militiamen into the creek stayed there, their blood intermingling with the brown water to turn it red.

Grizz Harvey fired as he had done before, picking his targets and putting them down. Beside him, Linc took his last grenade, pulled the pin and threw it at the creek bank. "Frag out!"

The explosion ripped through the undergrowth, killing and maiming those in its vicinity. On the far side of MacBride, the shortest man of the team at six-one, Nemo Kent, the group's designated marksman, worked as methodically as his commander with his Heckler & Koch 417.

"Eagle One, Delta One, copy?"

"Copy, Delta One, over."

"We've got a bird five mikes out from the LZ. Suggest you get your asses moving before you miss your ride. The client wants to know if you still have the package?"

The diamonds. That was all they cared about.

"Tell him we fucking lost them," Linc said over the open net.

"Say again, Eagle One."

Harvey ground his teeth together before answering, "Inform our client we still have his Blood Diamonds. Over."

"Damn it, Grizz," the operator on the other end shot back, perplexed.

"Whatever."

"You were told not to look."

"Fuck you too. You're not the ones out here getting shot at. How many people died for these things?"

"It's not your job to ask," a second voice came on the line. "Just to follow fucking orders, Harvey."

"Fuck you, Bennett. When was the last time you were down range? That's right, never."

The rest of the team glanced at each other while they kept up a good rate of fire. Just when things couldn't get any worse, they did.

"That's it," Bennett growled. "You're done. When you get back you can hit the road."

"Fine by me. Linc, throw the *package* into the creek."

"On it, boss."

"Wait," Bennett blurted out. "You can't do that."

Harvey watched as Linc did his thing. "Just did. Eagle One out."

Bennett came back shouting over the comms, but Harvey ignored him. Instead, he changed the channel and said, "Fuck you."

Linc said, "What are we going to do now?"

"If we get out of here alive, I'm retiring to Greece."

"Why Greece?"

"It's as far away from that fuck Bennett as I can get. Now, move out. Everyone, fall back to the LZ."

# CHAPTER THREE

FORMER GENERAL, now Team Reaper commander, Mary Thurston, walked into her commander's office early on the gray, windswept afternoon. She wore jeans and a jacket to keep out the chill. Her long dark hair was pulled back in a ponytail which hung down her back.

"You wanted to see me, sir?"

Hank Jones nodded. He pointed at a vacant chair opposite him and said, "Take a seat, Mary."

She sat down and looked around Jones' office. Never one for the material things in life the room was sparsely furnished. "Been decorating I see, sir."

He opened his mouth to speak but stopped when he saw the smile on her face. He grunted and leaned back in his chair. The Norman Schwarzkopf Jr. look-alike gave her a stern look.

"Come on, Hank, lighten up."

"If you say so. How are things?"

"Good. The team is on R&R, so it gives me a chance to catch up on things. Do you have a mission for us?"

"Not for the team, Mary. For you."

She frowned. "I'm intrigued."

"What have you heard about Medusa?"

"The sex trafficking cartel?" she asked.

"That's them."

"Just that they're named after Medusa because they have tentacles in many countries like she has snakes on her head."

Jones nodded. "Yes, and their activity continues to grow. It's believed they are behind at least six disappearances every day in Europe alone. It certainly works out to be big dollars. European girls and American girls seem to be all the rage this year. Two German girls turned up in Saudi Arabia last week. They'd been missing for nine months. They somehow managed to escape their owner and get to the British embassy in Riyadh. They were held there with a young British woman."

Jones slid a picture across the desk for Thurston to look at. The young woman was in her early twenties, blonde hair, blue eyes. "Natasha Holland. Twenty-one, from Birmingham. She was a student. Went to France seven months ago and disappeared. Along with her boyfriend. His body was found in the Seine River a week later."

"Quite attractive."

Jones grunted. He followed that picture with another. This one in stark contrast to the other. When Thurston saw it, her face grew grim.

"This is her when she was found the day after the two German girls reappeared. She was discovered with four others. Interpol is still trying to put names to them all, but it looks like the escape of the German girls sealed the fate of the others. Authorities raided the estate of Hakim Anwar and found nothing. This is why."

"Son of a bitch," Thurston growled. She leaned closer

to the picture before picking it up and studying it. "What's that mark?"

A third photo came across the desk. Thurston looked at it. The photo was a zoomed in version of the one before, showing clearly the mark of Medusa. Her head snapped up. "They brand them?"

"It looks that way."

"Assholes."

"That's a nice way of putting it."

"Do the German girls know what happened to the other girl?" Thurston asked.

Jones shook his head. "No, it was withheld from them and kept out of the media. They've already been through enough."

The Team Reaper commander nodded. "I gather you want Reaper to go after them?"

"No. I said this was a mission for you. Not the team."

"I don't understand. To get these people we'll need a team."

Jones nodded. "I'll get to that. MI6 came to me after the Prime Minister saw the same picture you just did. They want these people put out of commission. They told the PM they would 'look into it'. At the moment with budget constraints as they are, there is no financial allowance for a dedicated team to go after them. So, they came to us."

"I'm still not with you, Hank. You don't want our team doing it so that ultimately leads to finding another from somewhere."

He nodded. "Exactly. That's what I want you to do. Use all the resources at your disposal and get a team together that can work independently of the others. You'll need a strong commander which I'm sure you don't need to be told. Whoever you pick will answer to you, but you won't be hands-on like you are with Team Reaper. There's only one of you and you're needed with them."

31

Thurston was taken aback a little. "H—how big a team are we talking?"

"Whatever you feel you need. They'll have full use of the resources here at Global."

She thought about it for a while before saying, "I'll get Slick to find me some candidates. Do you have any preference?"

"Yes, don't get me a damn Brit guy like the last one."

Thurston smiled at the mention of Knocker. The man was a damn good soldier and Jones knew it. But he had a way of rubbing authority the wrong way. She nodded. "Fine, no Brits."

Jones grunted once more. "Get to it, Mary. And good luck."

———

THURSTON STOPPED when she opened the last folder she'd been furnished. Up until now the passel of files chosen as likely candidates for the new team had been borderline. But the last one was taking it over the edge. Rubbing a hand over her face at the lack of decent options, she looked up at Raymond "Knocker" Jensen and said, "What's this?"

"You said you wanted the best; that is the best."

"They're all discards," she shot back at him. "Hank Jones said no Brits but here I am, reading over the file of the biggest discard Brit of the lot."

Sam "Slick" Swift looked down at his feet like some child being scolded for doing something wrong. Not Knocker, though. He wasn't about to back down from this fight. Not when he thought he was right.

"I know this guy. He's from the Regiment. He's a damned good operator."

"Going by his file he can't follow orders."

"If you read the file carefully, you'll see that he follows the ones that count."

Thurston had to admit, the man selected for lead agent was seemingly good at his job. But he was British, which went against everything Jones had demanded.

"Ma'am," Knocker continued, "you asked us to find you people. Those are it. You get last say, sure. But if you take the time to study each file, you'll know we've picked some good people."

"One of them is in a federal prison," Thurston pointed out while arching an eyebrow.

It was Slick who spoke up this time. "He's good, ma'am. Not quite as good as me but close enough to scrape some paint off."

Thurston sighed as she stared at the stack of files. Her eyes flicked up to stare at Knocker. "All right. You and me tomorrow. Pack your toothbrush."

"What?"

"I'm going to need to see them. You're coming with me."

Knocker smiled. "Cool, road trip."

"It's not a road trip," she shot back at him.

"Do we get to share a room?" His look was hopeful.

"Shut up, Raymond."

———

*Berlin, Germany*

Anja Meyer sipped her coffee and studied the people on the street from the safety of the double-glazed café window. Her drink was strong, bitter, black. She checked her watch. It was a little past ten in the morning.

"Would you like some more coffee, Miss?" the waiter asked.

Anja put her hand over the top of her cup and shook her head. "No, thank you."

He smiled at her and moved on to the next table.

Anja's gaze drifted around the small café, stopping when it got to a table three over where two suited men sat. Things appeared to be quite kosher as they talked and laughed between themselves. But she knew better. Both men were linked to Viktor Medvedev. One was a courier. The other was a lieutenant in the organization.

Anja reached down and touched the gun tucked into the waistband of her pants. It had taken time, but she was close to getting the man responsible for ruining her career.

Suddenly the pair got up to leave. They walked past Anja, both smiling.

Counting to ten, she made to rise herself, intending to follow them. As she stood she came face to face with a woman with long dark hair. "Leaving so soon? Take a seat."

Anja glanced hurriedly over Thurston's shoulder. "I need to go."

Knocker stepped in beside her. "Take a seat, love. And don't try for the gun."

Anja turned her gaze on the Brit. "My name is not Love."

Thurston said, "Can we just talk to you for a moment, Anja? Please?"

"You know my name?"

"Amongst other things."

With a sigh of frustration, Anja sat back down. "I hope you know what you just did."

Thurston placed a folder on the table and opened it. "Anja Meyer, thirty-four and former head of a team for the Federal Intelligence Service. Kicked out after losing half of her team on an op. Harshly done by if you ask me."

"Anything else?"

"You were good at your job. Very good in fact. Which is why I'm here."

Anja stared at her in silence. "Who are you?"

"My name is Mary Thurston," Thurston continued. "I want to offer you a job."

Suddenly Anja was surprised. Then came the skepticism. "Me? A job?"

"Yes. I'm putting together a team and you came up as someone more than qualified to lead it."

"What about my past *indiscretion*?" she asked bitterly.

"I don't care about that. Your file speaks for itself."

"I already have a job," Anja said.

"Stalking the ones who put you out of a job? Doesn't pay the bills. I'm offering you a contract which pays two-hundred thousand American dollars per year."

"What the hell?" Knocker blurted out.

"Shut up, Raymond."

That got her attention. "What will I be doing?"

"Like I said, I'm putting a team together. It will be your team to command. I will be your immediate superior, but ninety-five percent of the decision making will be yours. Anything you need will be supplied by the company I work for."

"What company is that?'

"The Global Corporation."

Anja stared at her for a moment. "I think I've heard of you. A team you lead. You do good work."

"We try."

"What do you want me to do? You never really answered the question."

"Have you ever heard of Medusa?"

Anja nodded slowly. "Who hasn't? The worst trafficking ring across the globe."

"Your team will start with them."

"You keep saying team. What team?"

"At the moment it's just you."

"If I take it, can I request someone to work with me?"

"If I think they fit," Thurston replied.

"Ilse Geller. She's an intelligence officer from my old team. She's very good."

"I'll look into it. Does that mean you'll take the job?"

Anja thought for a moment thinking about what her new position could do for her. She nodded. "Yes."

Thurston smiled and slid an envelope across the table. "Expense money to get you by. I expect you to be in Hereford by the end of the week. The address is in there as well. All accommodation will be supplied. Welcome aboard."

———

*Greece*

"You're blocking my sunlight; fuck off," Grizz Harvey said curtly without opening his eyes.

In the background the sound of small waves lapping the beach had a soothing effect on the big man as he took in the rays of the Med. The beach was pristine, just about the last place you'd expect to find a former gorilla of special warfare.

"Grizz Harvey?" Thurston asked, remaining where she stood.

The big man sat up and removed his cheap ten Euro sunglasses. "Who wants to know?"

"Former general Mary Thurston."

"Former?"

"That's what I said."

"Who's your friend?"

"Ray Jensen. Formerly of Her Majesty's Special Air Service, now member of Team Reaper."

"Team Reaper?"

Knocker looked at Thurston. "Big feller is hard of

hearing, isn't he? Bet if you said you wanted to suck his cock he'd read you loud and clear."

"Hey, fuck you," Harvey snapped.

"Not today, Josephine. Looking at those muscles, I'd say something definitely suffered from your overuse of steroids."

Harvey took a step forward. "Let's go, Limey. I'll—"

"All right knock it off," Thurston snapped. "If you're Grizz Harvey, I'm here to offer you a job."

"What kind of job?"

"One that you excel at. Kicking doors."

"I'm listening."

"I need an experienced team of shooters for tough jobs. Kind of like a quick reaction force or backup if and when it's needed. I want you to command that team."

"You got a team in mind?" Harvey asked.

"No. I was hoping you might."

"I can get one."

"Fine. Next, are you going to have any issues taking orders from a woman?"

"I've heard of you. No, I don't think so."

Thurston smiled. "It won't be me you'll be taking orders from. But I will tell you this, she's experienced in command, and she won't take your shit. In return, she'll walk through hell to back you up."

"What's her name?"

"Anja Meyer."

"Sounds foreign."

"German."

He stared at her for a little longer. "All right. I'm in." He raised his arms indicating his surrounds. "Not like I'm doing much here anyway."

"Nice spot by the way," Knocker said.

Harvey glared at him. "What's wrong with it."

The Brit feigned innocence. "Nothing. I was just saying it was a nice spot."

"Uh huh."

"For bald-headed panty sniffers such as yourself."

"Son of a—"

Thurston stepped forward and slapped Harvey across his tattooed chest with an envelope. "Here. Expense money. I want you and your team in Hereford by the end of the week."

Harvey glared at Knocker once more before taking the packet, saying, "Yes, ma'am."

Thurston turned away and started across the beach, Knocker beside her. She looked at him and growled, "You just couldn't help yourself, could you?"

"Not in this lifetime, ma'am."

———

*Pine River Federal Correctional Facility, Virginia*

"Get up, shitbird. You got visitors."

Jimmy Garcia rolled off his bunk and came erect. The big guard stared at him with a look of utter disdain.

"Someone screw your wife again, Percy?"

The guard took a threatening step forward which caused Jimmy to leap back. "Keep pushing it, punk, and I'll put you in with the ladyboys."

Jimmy held up both hands in surrender. "All right, Percy, you got me. I apologize for anything that I may have said about your wife."

"Yeah, right."

"I must admit, she was a good screw."

"Son of a bitch." He lunged forward.

"Guard!" The voice was female, full of authority. Percy stopped.

Jimmy looked past the man mountain and he saw an attractive woman with long dark hair staring at him. "We'll take it from here."

"Yes, ma'am."

The guard stepped out of the cell to make room for the two visitors. "I'll be right outside, ma'am."

"Thank you."

They entered the cell and Jimmy took a step forward, smiling. Thurston held up a hand and said, "Before your mouth starts writing checks your body can't cash, let me give you some advice. See this big guy with me? He will rip your tongue out and stuff it down your throat. Got it?"

Jimmy nodded as he swallowed hard. "Yes, ma'am."

"Right. Jimmy Garcia, twenty-one, computer nerd."

"I prefer to call myself—"

Knocker stepped forward.

"Nothing at all," Jimmy finished.

"You hacked the FBI server. Why?" Thurston asked.

"I was bored."

"And look where that got you. Ten years for a little fun."

"Is there a point to this?" Jimmy asked.

"How would you like to get out of here?" Thurston asked.

Excitement flickered across his face. "What do I have to do?"

"Come and work for me in England."

Jimmy shook his head. "I can't. I have a home. Friends."

"Enjoy your ten years, kid," Knocker said as they both turned to leave.

"All right! All right! I'll do it."

Thurston stared at him. "If you screw up, try to run, anything that I don't agree with, you'll be back here in under forty-eight hours. Understood?"

"Yes, ma'am."

"Fine. Someone will have you out of here by the end of the day. I'll see you in Hereford."

The door shut behind them and as they walked along

the hallway, Knocker said, "Harvey will eat him for breakfast."

"Only if he gets up early enough to beat Anja to it."

The Brit chuckled. "One more to go."

"Yes, one more."

# CHAPTER FOUR

*Singapore*

HAWK RAN his gaze across the room taking in all that he could with one pass. Behind him coming through the door stepped Long Gen, head of the Jade Triad, one of Singapore's many drug cartels. He stopped behind Hawk and waited for him to give the all clear. Even though the club was Gen's, with the uptick in cartel violence of late one couldn't be too careful.

Behind Gen came three more men, all Singaporean. Hawk turned to his boss and nodded. Gen pushed past him and started to walk to the far side of the club's main floor past the twin pole-dance stages to a large booth. Hawk hated it. The thing was a death trap. When he first started bodyguarding for the cartel boss he told him straight out, don't go there. Gen had ignored him.

The cartel boss sat in the corner and waved his hand at the club manager. Within a minute, two of the club's most coveted girls appeared and slid into the booth beside the fat millionaire. Hawk on the other hand, went to the bar.

"What you want tonight, Jake?" the bar manager asked.

"Give me a Coke."

"What you want in it?"

"Captain Morgan."

It was going to be a long night. He leaned his back against the bar and began scanning the floor for any threats.

The first three rums went down without touching the sides, the next three almost the same. Come eleven, Hawk was drunk. Every night was the same. The booze was supposed to help blank out the dreams, the memories. Instead, it exacerbated things. So, what started out as drinking to forget progressed to drinking to numb the pain. Then it just became drinking.

"Fuck it," he said and ordered another.

One of the girls came up to him, her dark hair hung down her back and across her shoulders covering her small breasts. She said, "Jake, you want to take me to your room tonight?"

He stared at her through hazy eyes. He looked her up and down before saying, "Trixie?"

"Yeah, Jake. It me. You want good time tonight?"

"Do I look drunk to you?"

"Smashed."

"Then, sweetheart, you'd better find someone who can get it up."

"Never stop you before." She reached for his crotch and started to massage it. "See."

He leaned forward and kissed her. "Maybe that's all I needed. That and another drink."

"No, Jake, no. Let's go to your room."

"Maybe later, sweetheart."

Trixie huffed and stormed off while Hawk turned and ordered his next drink that he didn't really need.

"HE LOOKS LIKE A DRUNK," Thurston said. "Let's get out of here."

"Give him a chance," said Knocker. "I do some of my best work drunk."

"We're not talking screwing, Raymond. Besides, the guy works as a bodyguard for a cartel boss. Why wasn't that in the file?"

"Maybe we left that bit out."

"You'd better be able to explain that."

"Yeah, well. Can I finish my beer first?"

Knocker looked around the room and saw six men enter the club. They walked over to the girl that had been talking to Hawk. She was animated for a minute or so and then pointed at Hawk. "Heads up."

"What's the matter?" Thurston asked.

Knocker tipped his beer out and then turned the bottle upside down in his grip. "I'm not sure but I'm wishing I had my SIG about now."

As he watched, he slid off his stool and began circling through the crowd. That was when he saw the weapons. Just before things went south.

———

HAWK SAW them too and sobered almost instantly. Adrenaline coursed through his veins, clearing the haze that clouded his mind. He reached under his jacket and felt the butt of the Glock. He muttered a curse under his breath. He knew who they were and why they were here. Their target was Gen, but to reach him they had to get past Hawk. Hence, their approach to the former SAS man. This was not the place for a gunfight. Too many innocent people. But it was going to happen whether he liked it or not.

"Shit."

Hawk cleared the weapon and fired his first two shots into the ceiling above his head. Screams erupted as people began to scatter. Panic filled the room. The shooters were taken aback by his preemptive action, which gave Hawk an advantage.

He brought down the Glock and shot the first shooter in the head. The second shot did the same, while the third tore through the throat of the next would-be killer in line, spraying warm blood across the room.

But six was always going to be a stretch and by the time Hawk had brought down the fourth shooter, the fifth and sixth had their guns out and working. Both were armed with CZ Scorpion Evo 3s. Hawk leaped over the bar, the buzz of angry hornets chasing him. He disappeared leaving the bullets to hammer into the rear wall, smashing glasses, bottles, a mirror. Glass fell onto him like rain from an afternoon tropical storm.

Hawk ground his teeth together muttering curses to himself. He dropped out the partially spent magazine and replaced it with another.

With a look of grim determination etched on his face, Hawk came erect and took aim at the first of the remaining two shooters. His finger took up the minimal slack on the trigger until he suddenly released it.

"What the fuck?"

He looked on in amazement as some guy with a beer bottle came up behind the two men and smashed it over Hawk's intended target.

The shooter dropped to the floor, out cold. The bottle shattered leaving the attacker with only the neck in his hand.

The attacker moved quickly, utilizing the viciously jagged remains to his advantage. He stabbed it into the second shooter's throat and ripped it forward, severing the main artery.

Blood spurted from the ragged wound and the shooter dropped his weapon and grabbed at his throat in a futile attempt to stem the flow. The stranger then hit the shooter in the side of the head and dropped him beside his friend.

Through the mayhem Hawk saw a woman. Instead of running away from the trouble, she was pushing forward through the crowd. He saw her bend and pick up one of the Scorpions. Unsure, the former SAS man raised his weapon once more.

Before he could center his weapon on the woman, the guy who'd taken down the last two shooters stepped in front of him. "Hold your fire, Mate!"

Hawk released the trigger before the weapon could discharge. "Who are you?"

"A friend."

"Knocker?"

"Yeah."

Hawk looked around and saw that Gen and his body-guards had disappeared once the shooting started. "Fucking assholes."

"You want to leave before the constabulary start nosing around?"

Hawk nodded. "You and your friend follow me."

He led them out the back into a debris-strewn alley. He looked around and swore. "There goes the ride. Looks like we're on foot."

"We've got wheels," Thurston said.

"Where?"

"Out front."

"Not much good to us out there. Let's go."

Thurston glared at Knocker. The Brit gave a shrug and turned to follow Hawk. She shook her head and looked at the Scorpion still in her right hand. She threw it on a pile of garbage and started to follow the two men.

––––––

THE APARTMENT WAS SOMEWHERE between a cave and a sewer. Thurston took in the general disgusting state of the place before wrinkling her nose at the smell. She said, "Nice place."

"It's a shit hole," Hawk shot back at her.

"So why live here?"

"It's a good cover."

"From what?"

Hawk shook his head. "From whom. From most of the cartel figures throughout Singapore who want my head since the bounty was placed there by Gen."

"Wait," Knocker said. "The guy you work for put a bounty on your head?"

Hawk walked to the refrigerator and opened it. There were three shelves. Two were empty the other held a sixpack of beer. He took one and cracked the top. "You people want a beer?"

"No," Thurston replied. "Why did your boss put a bounty on your head?"

"He doesn't know it's me. Just someone the locals are calling Balas Dendam."

"What's that?" Thurston asked.

"The Revenger," Knocker told her.

Hawk nodded. "Someone started taking out members of the cartels, causing them to turn on one another. Gen put up the bounty to get whoever it was."

"Why?"

"Why what?"

"Why are you doing it?"

"I was hired to do it."

"By who?"

Hawk shook his head. "Let's just say it's political."

"So you've crossed to the dark side and become an assassin?" Knocker asked.

"Man's got to eat."

"And drink," Thurston retorted.

"Keeps the wolves at bay," Hawk lied taking another pull of his beer.

"Let's go," Thurston said to Knocker.

"Wait," Hawk said. "You're obviously here for something."

"I was looking for a lead agent in a new team I'm putting together. Jacob Hawk came to the top of the list."

"You seem to know my name, and possibly all about me or you wouldn't be here. But I know nothing about you."

"I'm Mary Thurston, and Ray you know. We work for Global Corporation."

"Out of Hereford?"

"That's right."

"I've heard of you. The US team now working in the private sector."

Thurston ignored him. "Like I said I'm looking for a lead agent for a new team. But I'm clearly making a mistake here."

"What doing?"

"I beg your pardon?"

"What's the team doing?"

"Taking down Medusa," Knocker said drawing a glare from his boss.

"Going big. I'm in."

"Why?"

"If you know so much about me you also know I was in the middle of a cock-up operation over a year ago when the young woman I was sent to get out went sideways. She was drugged to the hilt with enough Coke that she overdosed. She had a little tattoo on her. I didn't know what it was at first. Not until after. I found out that it was the mark of Medusa. So, I'm in."

Thurston stared at him. "If I take you and you turn out to be nothing more than a burned out drunk, don't worry about the bad dreams you're having. I'll shoot you in the head and it'll be over for you."

"Understood."

"Get your shit together. We leave now."

"I'm ready when you are."

"Yeah, we'll see."

———

*Mexico*

Maya Jones sat shivering in the corner of the small, dank room. Her side hurt from the tattoo applied to her by the masked man while the others had drugged and held her down. When she'd first been taken, she'd thought it to do with who her father was. Eli Jones, Texas oil billionaire. However, after the first days of her captivity and then the indignity of being tattooed, she'd been forced to rethink, realizing that it was more than that. Much more.

Then they had taken Jackson. She'd asked them where he'd gone but they refused to say. If only they'd stayed home for vacation instead of coming down to Mexico.

It was the middle of the day when they had been taken off the street. They'd been in a Mustang convertible outside of Mexico City when they were picked up.

The kidnap crew had been watching them for several days before moving in. Like the movies, they'd used a van. Had simply run them off the road, after which it was over in moments. Both Maya and Jackson were tied, bagged, and bundled into the back.

Never had she felt so far from home in Galveston than she did now.

The lock on the steel door rattled and it swung open. The hinges screeched in protest as metal ground on metal. Two men appeared. Each wore ski masks to hide their identities. "Stand up," one of them ordered, his voice accented. Definitely Mexican.

Maya shook her head. "No."

"Get up or we'll get you up," directed the second man. This one had a different accent. Maybe European.

"No, I—"

They walked forward and Maya forced herself harder into the corner. "Stay away from me."

"There's two ways of doing this. Now stand up."

"No."

The European looked at his companion. "You got it?"

The Mexican nodded and held up a syringe. "Right here."

"No, stay away from me. Stay away."

The European chuckled. "Don't worry. You won't feel a thing. And when you wake up—well, you'll wake up."

Maya let out a shriek as they closed in on her.

# CHAPTER FIVE

*Hereford, England*

HAWK LEANED FORWARD when the three women entered the operations room. Thurston he knew but the other two were strangers to him. Already he'd been introduced to Harvey and his team as well as the kid, Jimmy Garcia. "I wonder who they are?" he whispered to Harvey.

The big operator said, "I'm guessing one of them is our new boss."

"New boss?"

Harvey nodded. "Yes, didn't Thurston tell you?"

"No."

"Her name is Anja Meyer. She's German. When I found out I did some asking around. She was once the head of a specialist team in the German Federal Intelligence Service."

"Any good?"

"Very," Harvey replied. "Right up until half of her team got killed and a bomb went off in Berlin."

"I bet she got a bollocking for that."

"Sure did."

"Who is the other cow?"

Harvey frowned. "Cow?"

"Term of endearment, mate."

"I see. I don't know who she is."

"She's hot, boss," Nemo Kent whispered to them.

"Shut it, Nemo."

"Listen up," Thurston said. "Gather around and we'll get started."

Everyone moved forward so they weren't so far away. Thurston continued. "All right. This is Anja Meyer. She is your new boss. From now on you answer to her. If you fuck up in any way she has full authority to kick your asses out the door. Understood?"

Her eyes focused on Hawk. "Understood?"

He nodded. "Yes, ma'am."

"Good. I'll hand you over to her."

Anja straightened. When she spoke, her accent was thick. "I have read files on each of you. Not the most flattering reads I have ever experienced. However, let's look upon this as a second chance. For all of us."

They all gave slight nods.

"We will operate as an autonomous unit. Home is wherever we are at the time. Our goal is to shut down the operation known as Medusa."

Hawk put up his hand. Anja looked at him. "Yes, Jacob?"

"What are ROEs in foreign countries and what happens if we get caught on the wrong side of the law?"

"Rules of engagement are standard and to answer your second question, we play the hand we're dealt."

"Not instilling me with a lot of confidence, ma'am."

"Miss Meyer."

Hawk raised his eyebrows. "Pardon?"

"You will address me as Miss Meyer."

Beside him, Harvey choked back a chuckle. Hawk glanced at Thurston and saw her unmoved. "You want me to call you Miss Meyer?"

"Not want. If you are to be part of this team where I am in charge you will call me Miss Meyer. In return I will call you Jacob."

He stared at her, his rage beginning to boil inside. But the longer he looked at her expression he realized she wasn't challenging him nor trying to assert her authority over him; it was simply what she wanted done. He nodded. "All right. Miss Meyer it is."

Then she smiled. "Thank you, Jacob. I shall look forward to working with you. Do any of you have a problem with this arrangement?"

The four operators glanced at each other. Harvey cleared his throat. "If it's an order, ma'am, we'll follow it."

"It's not an order, Mister Harvey. It is just what I call a sign of respect for the chain of command."

"Yes, ma'am. Ah—Miss Meyer."

Hawk looked at the big bald operator and grinned. Then mouthed the word, "Pussy."

It was returned by a "Fuck you."

"Is there anything else before we continue?" Anja asked.

"Ma'am—Miss Meyer," Harvey corrected. "My team will need weapons and equipment."

"Do you have a preference?"

"As long as it works and doesn't jam while we're in the middle of a firefight would be good."

"CZ Bren Two?"

Harvey nodded. "That'll work."

"A DMR as well?" she asked, meaning a designated marksman rifle.

"That would be good, ma'am. I mean Miss Meyer."

"Light machine gun, grenades, suppressors, satellite comms, NVGs?"

"We'll take whatever you can throw at us," Harvey replied.

"Get a list to me after the briefing and I'll see that you get it before we are deployed." Anja looked at Thurston who nodded. "What about you, Jacob?"

"Just as long as it goes bang, I'm good."

Thurston stared at Jimmy. "I'll hook you up with my team tech and he'll fix you for equipment."

"Thank you, ma'am."

Anja went on, indicating to the woman who stood slightly behind her. She was fine featured, and her mousy colored hair was tied back. "This is Ilse Geller. She is our intelligence officer. She will brief you on missions and anything else that is required."

They all nodded at her, saying hello. She smiled warmly. Jimmy said, "Do we call her Miss Geller?"

Hawk reached out and slapped him up the back of his head.

"Ouch, what did you do that for?"

Anja ignored them. "Understand this. We are not the sledgehammer that gets things done. We are a surgical strike team. Instead of bludgeoning them to death, we'll cut their hearts out. Mister Harvey and his men will be used only when I deem it necessary. Our main weapons will be intelligence and Mister Hawk."

"Kicking doors is what we do," Harvey pointed out.

Anja nodded. "And there will come a time for exactly that. I'm fully expecting Mister Hawk to attract trouble like flies to manure. But our primary role for this mission is extraction."

"Hang on a minute," Hawk said. "I thought we were after Medusa."

"That's right, we are."

"Now I'm confused."

"Something has come up which has to take precedence. Ilse will explain."

Ilse stepped forward and a picture came up on the big screen. "This is Maya Jones and Jackson Foster. Just over a week ago they disappeared in Mexico. Maya's father is oil tycoon Eli Jones. When they first disappeared, it was thought to be a kidnapping and a ransom demand was expected. One never came. Instead, this was found."

A picture of a corpse was shown floating in a creek.

"That is Jackson. He was shot in the back of the head and dumped. Two days earlier, his car was found outside of Mexico City. It had been run off the road into a ditch. It is assumed this is the point that they were captured."

"Cartels?" Harvey asked.

Ilse shook her head. "We don't think so. I've been working up a brief for the past ten hours and it seems that within the past two months, up to ten girls have disappeared around Mexico City. Each has been American."

"That seems to be an awful lot," Hawk said.

"We have intel on a pipeline running from Mexico to a market in Brazil where various people will pay top dollar for a certain type of girl."

"Do we know who is running the pipeline?" Hawk asked.

"Not yet. But if we find the girl then we find those responsible."

"Could it be Medusa?" Harvey asked.

"It's possible but we won't know until we get there."

"When do we leave?"

Ilse looked at Anja. "Tonight. Don't expect to be back here for a while."

"Hey, what are we called?" Nemo Kent asked. "We've got to have a cool name."

Anja stared at them for a moment before saying, "Talon."

Nemo smiled. "I like that."

"Everyone get ready. Jacob, a word."

Hawk waited while Thurston and Anja discussed final preparations. Once they were done, she left, and Anja turned her attention to the former SAS man. "I'm relying on you to get results."

Hawk nodded. "I'll do my best."

"I need more than your best. You'll be in the field on your own. I need to know I can count on you."

"You can."

"All right. Once we board the flight to Mexico, I'll discuss the operation more with you."

"Yes, ma'am."

She stared at him. Hawk shook his head. "Are we really going to do this?"

The stare lingered.

"Yes, Miss Meyer," he managed. "One thing. I hate Jacob. Just call me Jake, all right?"

She nodded. "All right, Jake."

"And I'll call you Anja."

"No, you won't."

"Shit."

"I'll see you on the plane."

He grinned at her. "Yes, ma'am.

———

"ARE we really going to call her Miss fucking Meyer, Grizz?" asked Linc Sheffield. "It makes me think I'm back at fucking school."

Harvey examined his Bren and gave a shrug. "She's the boss. Just think of it as saying sir and ma'am. Or captain even."

"Somehow, it just don't set right."

Harvey's gaze flicked to each of his men. There were times when you backed your men and there were times when you set them straight. This was one of those times.

"All right, listen up. That woman is our CO. So if she wants to be called Miss Meyer, then that is what we call her. Shit, we'll call her Mary Fucking Poppins if she wants. While I'm in command of this team you'll do as I say. Or you can find the nearest door and walk through it. Understood?"

They all nodded. "Get your kit ready."

Each of them wandered away to do as they were ordered.

"Teething problems?" Hawk asked as he seemed to appear out of nowhere.

"No, just setting the record straight."

"What do you make of our new boss?"

"Like I said. From the intel I saw, she was good. Commanded a top-notch team."

"What else did you find out?"

"Such as?"

"What happened to her team?"

"Half of them died," Anja said from behind Hawk.

The former SAS man looked guiltily at Harvey and mouthed the word 'Fuck'. Hawk turned and started to give an explanation. "Look, I'm—"

Anja held up a hand and stopped him. "Do not explain. It is natural that you wish to know more about me. After all, your life is basically in my hands."

"All right," said Hawk. "What happened?"

She told him from start to finish.

"What happened to Medvedev?" Hawk asked.

"The same as what happened to Lars Akker," she replied.

He grunted. "Fuck all."

"In a nutshell."

"Well, I'll make you this deal. You do right by us, and we'll do right by you."

Anja stared into his eyes and could see he was speaking the truth. Then she looked at Harvey who gave her the same look. He said, "It's all a part of being a team, Miss Meyer, as you already know."

"I'll hold you to that."

"I wouldn't have it any other way."

"Ma'am," Hawk said, his gaze giving away what he was about to say.

Anja nodded. "All right. A new beginning all around. While we are working you can call me ma'am or boss. When we are not then you may call me by my first name. But I expect my orders to be followed at all times. Am I clear?"

"Yes, ma'am."

"Fine. Wheels up in an hour."

———

"LOOKS like we're flying in style," Hawk said to Harvey as they stared at the Bombardier Global 7500 aircraft.

Grizz Harvey looked troubled. "How the fuck are we meant to get all our equipment on that?"

"You're not," Anja said from behind them. "Thin it out to only what's necessary."

"What if it's all necessary?" Hawk asked.

"It won't be."

"I hope you're right."

———

*Over the Atlantic*

"Once we land, we'll go straight to the safehouse which is set up for what we need," Anja said to Hawk. "From there you'll head out on a lead which we have."

"What lead is that?"

The Talon commander looked over his shoulder. "Ilse, a moment."

"Yes, Miss Meyer."

She sat next to her boss opposite Hawk. In her hands was her laptop. Anja said, "The lead we have. Explain to Jake what it is."

She smiled at Jake and tapped a few keys on her computer. Without looking up she said, "There is a club in Mexico City I've been able to link through all the victims' social media accounts."

"Wait," Hawk said. "Why didn't the local coppers do this?"

"I think they did but because of who the owner is it may have been swept aside," Ilse explained.

"I'm not going to like this am I?" Hawk theorized. He sighed. "Tell me."

Ilse turned the laptop around and showed Hawk a picture of a handsome looking man with dark hair. "The owner is Cesar Lozano. Head of the Lozano Cartel. They're not big, but they do make up for it by being nasty."

"Could he have something to do with the disappearances?"

"He could but his main operation is drugs and kidnap for ransom."

Hawk nodded. "Which is different to what happened to the others."

"Yes."

"But to get answers I have to start somewhere, and this is it."

"Something like that."

"Are you sure about the intel? Could there be something else linking them?"

Ilse looked indignant before gathering herself. Anja said, "Jake, if Ilse says the intel is good, then rest assured that what she says is true. In all our years working together, I've never had cause to question the intel she supplied us. Even that which caused the death of half of my team."

Hawk looked at Ilse. "I'm sorry."

She nodded. "We are new to each other. There are bound to be times when you have questions."

"All right, tell me about the link."

Ilse turned the laptop and let her slender fingers dance once more. "Like I said, pictures from their social media accounts link each of them to the club. But that isn't all. In most there was a person who kept popping up. Not in all but in enough to make it more than a coincidence."

The computer swung back around, and Hawk was staring at another man. "Do we know who he is?"

Ilse shook her head. "Sorry. I even had Jimmy looking but there is nothing on him. It's like all record of him has been cleansed."

"Just the way a high-profile crime organization would want it, to remain in the shadows."

"Yes."

"All right. Next question. Seeing as it is a cartel situation, do the local cops know we're coming?"

"No," Anja replied with a shake of her head.

"Government?"

"No."

"Cover?"

Ilse said, "You'll be the usual tourist. I'll have you backstopped. You'll be using the name John Cameron. Jimmy will print you up all the documentation that you'll need before you step into the field."

Hawk chuckled. "A tourist with a gun instead of a camera."

The two women remained silent. The former SAS operator caught their hesitation. "You've got to be shitting me."

Anja said, "You can't carry a gun, Jake. That's the first thing that anyone will look for."

"And what if I need one?"

"I'm sure you'll improvise. Other than that, John and his team will be on standby."

"What do you mean by standby?"

"Maybe a couple of blocks out."

"Maybe a couple—I could do a lot of dying in that time."

"I'm certain a man of your expertise will cope just fine," Anja said. "And if you die, I promise to give you a decent burial and cry a little."

"Don't overdo yourself, boss."

"It will be no trouble. Now, Ilse will give you a file to look at so you can hit the ground running."

———

*Outside Mexico City*

The Global 7500 touched down on a concrete strip outside the city. One where the owner looked hard in the opposite direction if paid enough to do so.

The team unloaded their gear and took it all to a hangar at the edge of the field. Hawk looked around the large building and said, "I thought you said we were using a safehouse."

Anja shrugged. "Safehouse, safehangar, much the same."

She was dressed in a pair of faded jeans and a dark blue singlet top. On her thigh, like the rest of the team she had a holster containing a SIG Sauer P226 handgun. She removed her dark sunglasses and considered their surroundings. "John?"

"Yes, ma'am?" Harvey replied.

"Can you fetch the MP5s for myself and Ilse, please? Then set up a lookout just in case our friend who owns this dump decides he might be able to get some money for us."

"Yes, ma'am."

"Why don't I get an MP thingy?" Jimmy whined.

Anja stared at him. "Have you ever used one?"

"No—"

"John?"

"Yes, ma'am?"

"At some point would you have one of your men verse Mister Garcia in the use of that handgun on his thigh before he shoots himself in the foot?"

"I can do that," Harvey replied. He walked over to Jimmy and asked, "Is that weapon safe?"

"What do you mean by safe?"

The big man shook his head and took the weapon from its holster. He removed the magazine, the round from the chamber and then gave it back to Jimmy in pieces. "There, now it's safe."

Hawk smiled. "I can see this is just going to be the bee's knees."

The team got to work setting up and soon all was ready. Harvey had Linc and Kent on watch while Jimmy got a satellite link ready and the comms online. Meanwhile Ilse went over the final plan with Hawk. "Once you arrive on target, we should be able to monitor you through the satellite hookup. It will be live for an hour. If you need any more than that it'll be comms only."

"How am I meant to get into the city?" Hawk asked.

As though on cue in some well-rehearsed movie a vehicle appeared outside the hangar. A dark van. "John will drop you within walking distance of the club. That will be your base of operations while you're all in the city."

As he looked on, Anja walked over to the driver who had gotten out of the van. She held out an envelope which the man took and after a short exchange of words, he walked away.

"I guess that's our ride."

"Looks that way."

"It'll be good to get back to doing real work," Hawk said.

"You mean possibly getting shot at?"

"Makes you feel alive."

Ilse smiled. "Wonderful."

# CHAPTER SIX

*Mexico City*

IT DIDN'T TAKE MUCH to identify the heavy hitters both outside and within the club. So far Hawk had picked out eight, but he was sure that there were more than he'd found at a glance.

The music was loud but not unbearable. Young people filled the dancefloor jumping and grinding against each other. He figured their ages would average out maybe in the mid-twenties.

Bright lights flashed from the ceiling, strobing at a fast pace. Hawk felt naked without his personal weapon and wondered how long it would be before he had to use his intuition to save his own ass.

He looked at the back wall above the bar and saw three cameras. Two pointed along the bar in either direction while the third was pointed perpendicular to the wall itself.

Behind the counter four people served drinks. Three females, one male. The women all wore tight black T-shirts and black lipstick. They each had long dark hair flowing down their backs.

"You got eyes on me, Alpha One?" he said trying to cut through the noise.

"We've got you, Jake," Anja replied. "You could get them to turn the music down. Maybe play some Roxette or something."

Hawk smiled. "Like your older music, boss?"

"A conversation for another time."

"Yes, ma'am. Any sign of our mystery friend?"

"Negative."

"Well, I might get myself a drink and enjoy the evening."

"Remember, Jake, we lose the satellite in fifty minutes," Ilse reminded him.

"Well then, do you have any requests before the lights go out?"

The intelligence officer tried not to smile and glanced at Anja whose face was like stone. "Mind on the job at hand, Jake."

"You people are no fun."

Hawk waited for one of the girls to come to him. "What will it be, señor?"

"I'll have a beer, love."

She stared at him for a moment, her brown eyes smiling almost as much as her mouth was. "You are British."

It was a statement. "Sure am."

She grabbed him a bottle and he paid for it. Hawk asked when she brought the change back, "What do you do for fun around here?"

"Are you hitting on me, señor?"

Hawk returned her smile. "Me? No, I was just making polite conversation, love."

"Juanita."

He held a hand up to his ear. "What?"

"Juanita. That is my name."

"Hi. I'm John Cameron."

The barman walked past her and rattled off some words in Spanish. Juanita's smile disappeared and was replaced with uncertainty. "I will see you later, John Cameron."

Hawk held up his beer. "I hope so, Juanita."

He turned his back to the bar and looked across the room. A voice in his ear said, "What was that, Jake?"

"Just getting to know the locals."

"Get your damn head in the game." There was venom in her voice and for a moment Hawk was taken aback by it. This was a strong woman.

The former SAS operator walked across the room and found a table near the wall to sit at. Using his training he sat and took it all in. Eighty percent of the crowd were definitely Mexican. The balance was a combination of American, European, and numerous different countries.

"Heads up we've got movement."

"What's happening?" Hawk asked Ilse.

"A black SUV stopped out front. Five people just got out. One looks to be Cesar Lozano."

"That should make things interesting."

"What will?"

The former SAS operative looked up to see Juanita standing before him. "Pardon?"

"What will make things interesting? Who were you talking to?"

"Myself. I do it all the time." He looked past her towards the doorway and saw the small entourage enter. "Who's that?"

Juanita cast a glance over her shoulder. She licked her lips nervously and said, "It is the owner."

"What's his name?"

"I have to go back to work. I will come back later."

He nodded. "Sure."

Juanita disappeared and left Hawk to watch over the

new arrivals. A few minutes later, Ilse said, "You know how you said it was going to be interesting, Jake?"

"I remember saying something along those lines but don't quote me."

"Facial recognition just pinged off our person of interest."

"I knew I should have brought a gun."

———

*The Hangar*

"Is it a positive ID?" Anja asked, leaning over Ilse's shoulder.

"Yes, Miss Meyer. What do you want to do?"

"Jake, copy?"

"Roger."

"It's your call."

"We'll see how the ball bounces."

"All right, Jake, you're still in play." Anja turned to Jimmy. "I want to know what is beyond our perimeter. Can you do it?"

He gave a sharp nod. "Consider it done."

"Ilse, run facial recognition over the whole club. This time reset your parameters."

"Yes, Miss Meyer. Am I looking for anything in particular?"

"No. Let's see what pops."

"On it."

"Grizz, are you and Linc ready to go on my word?" Anja asked Harvey over his comms.

"Just say the word, ma'am."

"Stand by."

She looked at the screen and said to herself in a low voice, "Now, let's see how this works out."

"This isn't good," Hawk muttered to himself.

"What was that, Jake?" Ilse asked.

"Wait one. Stand by."

"Jake, talk to me."

As Hawk watched, he saw one of Lozano's heavies point out the target Talon was interested in. The cartel boss' expression changed noticeably as he spoke to his men. Two of them broke off immediately and approached the target who was standing at the bar.

Obviously not expecting trouble, he didn't see them until it was too late. By then he had a man crowding him on either side. He turned his head both ways, trying to work out if it was a casual contact, realizing that it was anything but casual.

Out of the dark recesses of the bar area another man appeared. Attired in black pants and a white singlet, his exposed arms and upper chest revealed whipcord muscle covered in a carpet of tattoos. He also wore a holstered handgun openly which told Hawk that the man thought himself a law unto no one.

"Alpha Two, I need an ID on the guy who just appeared."

"Give me a moment, Jake," Ilse replied.

The target was not so gently ushered by the three men, away from the bar towards the rear of the club. "He may not have a moment, Alpha Two. Grizz, you with me, cock?"

"Getting every word, Jake."

"Meet me around the back of the club."

"Roger that."

"Jake, what are you going to do?" Anja asked.

"Improvise."

Hawk rose from his seat taking the bottle of beer with him. As he walked through the crowd, he tipped it up and poured the remaining contents onto the floor. Once it was empty, he grasped it by the neck and kept walking.

"Jake, they've gone out into the rear of the club," Ilse said.

"Yeah, I saw them go. They left a guy standing guard outside the door."

As he approached the guard, Hawk changed his gait. Now he walked like he was drunk. The guard stepped in front of him, holding up a hand. "*Detente ahí.*"

Hawk squinted at him, making out he was confused. "What? You don't speak the Queen's English, wanker?"

The same confused expression was returned momentarily before the guard opened his coat to show the Brit his weapon. Then in accented English said, "Fuck off."

Hawk smiled at him, all signs of drunkenness gone. "No, you fuck off, mate."

The hand with the bottle in it came up and around in an unexpected blur of movement. It shattered against the side of the man's head and dropped him on the spot. Hawk quickly looked around before grabbing him by the collar and dragging him through the door and into the doorway beyond.

Over his comms he heard Ilse say, "That was brutal."

"He's lucky I wasn't mad."

Bending down Hawk removed the weapon from the man's shoulder holster. It was an FN Five-seven. He hurriedly checked it before stuffing it into his pants. Looking at the jagged edges of the shattered bottle remains in his hand, he considered its practicality. It wasn't a knife, but it would do for a silent kill if required.

"Jake, I've got an ID on tattoo man," Ilse said. "He's Pedro Carrillo. Top sicario for Lozano. He is former Mexican Special Forces. Killed his commanding officer and then disappeared. Reappeared as Lozano's head exterminator six months later. He's suspected in multiple killings and assassinations including those of three top judges."

"You need to be careful, Jake," Anja told him. "But we need that HVT out of there and able to talk."

"There's something else, Jake," Ilse added.

"Do I want to know?"

"I count maybe five more cartel soldiers who came with Carrillo. Once it starts, you need to exfil pronto."

"Wish me luck."

Hawk made his way along the short hallway with two doors. One was marked as the exit, the other, judging by the sounds coming from behind it, he was in the right place. Raised voices seemed to be the order of the evening.

Hawk put the broken bottleneck in his left hand and drew the FN with his right. He tapped the barrel on the door and waited.

———

THERE WERE seven people inside the room including the HVT wanted by Talon. The room itself was starkly bare: no cupboards, no table, just one chair on the concrete floor sitting over a drain cover.

Lozano strolled nonchalantly around the room, hands locked together behind his back. He stopped pacing suddenly and turned to stare down at the man on the chair. He took in the blood and cuts on the man's face inflicted by Carrillo, and seemed genuinely remorseful for having to treat the man in such a manner.

"Listen to me, hombre. You were told to stay away from my club."

"It's a good club," the man said weakly, his European accent evident.

"And I want it to stay that way. But because of you

and your people I am getting all kinds of attention. Did you not tell them I said to find another club?"

"I did," the man nodded. "And the truth is I'm more scared of them than I am of you."

A knife appeared in Carrillo's hand, the tip of it penetrating the skin below the man's right eye, eliciting a high-pitched shriek.

"Wait," Lozano snapped waving his hand at the knife-man. "I want to hear what else he has to say."

"My people want to meet you. Give you some compensation for the trouble you're experiencing. I came here to find you. but your goons grabbed me first."

"What kind of compensation?" the cartel boss asked. "I have all the money I need."

The man shook his head. "They didn't tell me. They said if you're interested there will be a vehicle waiting out the back for you."

That was when the tap came at the door.

Lozano looked at the man closest to the door, giving him a cold look. The goon turned and stepped over to the door to open it.

———

AS SOON AS the door was open far enough, Hawk's left hand streaked out and the broken bottleneck buried itself into the soft flesh of the unwary man's throat. He reeled back, blood gushing from the wound where the artery had been opened. Hawk kicked the door wide and stepped into the room.

His first two shots took down two of Lozano's body-guards. One shot each. BOOM! BOOM!. They fell to the floor and the Brit shifted his aim to cover Carrillo. "Nope. Don't do it, mate. I can squeeze the trigger quicker than you can fart in the wind."

As soon as he finished the statement Hawk shifted his

aim, placing a throat shot into one of the bodyguards who hadn't heeded the warning, before aiming once more at the sicario. "Told you."

"I fucking kill you, puta," Carrillo hissed. "You will never get out of Mexico City alive."

Hawk shrugged. "Yeah? Not going to happen." He shot him in the leg before shifting his aim to Lozano.

"You want one too? I have enough to go around."

"What do you want?"

Hawk indicated the man on the chair. "I'll take him."

*"Jake, you need to get out of there."*

"You good to go, old mate?" Hawk asked him.

"Who are you?"

*"Jake, now blast it."*

"Can you walk, or do I leave you here with them?"

"I can walk."

"Then get up."

"You are dead, gringo," hissed Lozano full of loathing.

"That's Mister Gringo to you."

Hawk took Carrillo's personal weapon and straightened. He stuffed it into his waistband and looked at his HVT. "Time to go."

The two men moved towards the door. "Talk to me, Alpha Two."

"You've got three men coming your way."

"Roger that. I've got the HVT with me. Grizz, you still with me?"

"Loud and clear, Jake."

"I'm going to be coming out in about two mikes."

"We'll be here."

As the two men entered the hallway, the three cartel shooters appeared. Hawk shoved the HVT backward as he brought up the FN handgun. Hawk fired twice and the first cartel man fell at the feet of his friends.

The second man in line opened fire with an automatic weapon and sprayed the hallway with a hailstorm of lead.

"Shit!" Hawk exclaimed as he threw himself back, landing on the hard floor and jarring every part of his body.

He scrambled backward, propelling himself with his legs. A shooter appeared in the doorway and the FN crashed twice more. The man cried out and fell forward. Hawk waited several moments, expecting the third man's face, but he failed to appear.

The Brit scrambled to his feet and looked around the room. He saw Lozano staring at him, his face a mask of rage. Carrillo on the other hand had moved towards one of the fallen bodyguards.

"Hey, you," he said to the man he was there to get. "What's your name?"

"Barry White."

"Yeah, fuck off," Hawk grunted. He reached for the spare handgun and passed the other one with the half-spent magazine to the man calling himself Barry. "Take this. If you need to, shoot them."

The man took the weapon and as Hawk turned back towards the door two shots crashed behind him. Startled he turned back to see both Lozano and Carrillo dead on the floor.

"Fuck me. What did you do that for?"

"They're better that way."

The third shooter from the hallway appeared, drawn out by the gunfire within the room. Hawk's weapon snapped up and he shot the man in the stomach. The shooter grunted and doubled over, his gun spilling from his hand.

"Come on, move," Hawk snapped.

The hallway was clear, and he said into his comms, "Grizz, we're coming out."

"We're still here, Jake."

The door flew open to the street and cool air rushed into the void bringing with it the rancid stench of decaying garbage. Hawk spotted the van and the door slid open to reveal Linc waiting for them. "Over here."

Suddenly a shot cracked, and the man called Barry grunted. He staggered and went down on one knee. "Sniper!" Hawk shouted and blew off five rounds from the handgun. "Across the street, second floor."

Linc came out of the van with his Bren2. He aimed at the window and opened fire. "Get him in the van."

Hawk grabbed the wounded man by the collar and dragged him towards the van. Barry moaned in pain, barely conscious. The Brit heaved him into the vehicle and called out to Linc. "He's in."

Linc fell back into the van. He slammed the door shut and called out, "Last man. Go! Go!"

Harvey trod on the gas pedal and the van shot forward. In the back, Hawk said, "I need some light."

Linc grabbed a small flashlight and shone it on the wounded man. Hawk ripped his shirt wide and saw the bullet hole gushing blood like a fast-flowing stream. "Fuck!"

He placed a hand over the hole and pressed down. Barry lurched violently and cried out in agony.

Hawk called, "I need something for this wound."

Linc took a large pad out of his pack. He placed it over the wound and Jake pushed down again. Another cry of pain, this one not as loud. Blood was pooling under the wounded man and around the knees of those trying to help him.

"Jake, what's going on?" Anja asked.

"There was a sniper, Alpha One. Our man took a round. He's bleeding out. He needs a doctor."

"Negative, Jake. Is he conscious?"

Hawk looked through the semi darkness at Linc. The man shrugged.

"Shit," Hawk muttered. "Only just, Alpha One."

"Get what you can out of him, Jake. We're not here,

remember. The police are already responding to the shooting. It won't be long before word gets out. You need to extract the information now."

"Yes, ma'am."

"What am I doing, Jake?" Harvey called back from the driver's seat.

"Back to base, Grizz. Floor the shit out of it."

"Roger that."

Hawk stared at the man on the van floor. He'd passed out from pain, and he guessed he wasn't far from death. "Wake him up, Linc."

The strike team's second in command patted Barry on the face. "Hey, wake up. Come on, buddy. Open those eyes. Talk to me."

Eyes fluttered open. "W—What?"

"Look at me, Barry," Hawk said. "Barry, you with me?"

"What?"

"Who do you work for?"

"N-no one."

"Come on, Barry, don't fuck with me. You and your friends took a girl and her boyfriend. Who are they?"

"D—don't—"

"I haven't got time for this shit, Barry. You're on your way to the great oven, mate. You're screwed. Where is the girl?"

The dying man coughed. Blood spilled from his lips and ran down his chin. His breathing was already growing shallow and his chest rattled.

"He's fucked up, Jake," Linc observed.

"Barry, listen to me. Tell me about the girl."

Barry's eyes brightened, his eyes darted left and right as though he was looking for something. He smiled weakly. "They—they—you can't get them."

His head lolled to the side.

"Barry? Get who Barry?" Hawk asked. "Barry, get who?"

"He's gone, Jake," Linc said stating the obvious.

"Fuck it," Hawk hissed and sat back. "Shit."

"Jake, look," Linc said.

Hawk leaned forward and saw what the flashlight beam was illuminating. A tattoo of a snake woman's head. Medusa.

"Sitrep, Bravo One?" Anja asked using Hawk's code-name for the first time.

"HVT is dead, Alpha One. The mission is a bust. Returning to base."

———

ANJA AND HAWK watched the body being retrieved from the van. She took him aside and asked, "What happened?"

"You were monitoring the radio. You work it out," he replied abruptly.

She stared hard at him. "Not the response I want, Jake."

"There was a sniper, all right? For some reason, and I don't know how, they were waiting for him."

Anja frowned. "I'll have Jimmy and Ilse look over everything. For now, get cleaned up and rested."

"There was one thing, ma'am."

"Yes?"

"There is a tattoo on him. The Medusa head."

"So they don't just do it to their captives," Anja replied.

"No, it looks like they put it on everyone they own."

She nodded grimly. "We need to find another lead."

# CHAPTER SEVEN

*The Hangar*

HAWK AND HARVEY watched the screen before them. The footage was of a burning vehicle surrounded by bodies. Some police and others were civilian. It cut to another video reel where a different civilian was firing an automatic weapon at two men behind a battered truck. Along the bottom of the feed on the ticker was the headline about fierce gun battles in the city as chaos descended upon it.

Harvey said, "One man dies, and this happens."

Hawk retorted defensively, "Not my fault. Besides, the world is a better place this morning."

"Never said it was."

Sensing a presence behind him, the Brit looked back and saw Anja standing there. "What's happening?"

"You don't know?"

"I haven't had time to see what's going on in the real world," she replied rubbing wearily at the back of her neck.

Hawk said, "You need to get some down time, boss."

"Soon. So what's going on?"

"It seems word got out about Lozano's death," Harvey explained. "It left a vacuum that other bad guys are rushing to fill. A war has started on the streets of Mexico City."

"That's all we need," she responded.

"What's going on?"

"Briefing in five minutes. Be there and you'll find out."

"Do we have something?"

"Five minutes," was all she said before turning and leaving.

———

THE TEAM CAME TOGETHER in less than four minutes, gathering around Ilse who started with her intelligence briefing. "Jimmy and I still haven't found out the identity of our dead mystery man. But we're still working on it. It looks like Medusa has scrubbed him clean. However, through sheer intelligence brilliance—" she glanced sideways at Anja whose face remained passive, "we've got a second person of interest."

"Who is he?" Hawk asked.

"He's a Mexican national, that much we do know. His name we're not sure of. However, we've tracked him here to this apartment complex." A picture of the complex appeared.

"Do we know what apartment?" Hawk asked.

"We're not sure," Ilse replied. "If we had a name, it would be easier."

"We doing surveillance?"

"No. You'll have to go in cold."

"What about transport? We using the van again?" Harvey asked.

"No," Anja replied. "Jake is going in on his own."

Hawk stared at the building. It was so rundown it was almost derelict, what paint was left was peeling, garbage was piled high around it everywhere. There was even a partially stripped vehicle in the parking lot.

Harvey stared at his boss, incredulity all over his face. "You can't send him in there alone."

"The place is in the middle of all the fighting," Ilse told the big man. "We can't send you all because you will stand out. One man should get in and out."

"It's too dangerous," Harvey persisted.

"Why don't we ask Jake?" Anja asked.

All eyes sought out the Brit who was peering intently at the picture. His eyes flicked to Ilse. "We have eyes upstairs?"

"Yes."

"So you can guide me in?"

"Yes, I can."

"What kind of bird?"

"A UAV. It can remain on station for the duration of the op."

"Armed?"

"No."

He looked at Anja. "I go armed this time." It was a statement not a question.

She nodded. "Take whatever you need. You'll be going in after dark. Between now and then we will try to nail down an address."

Hawk nodded. "I can do it."

"You're crazy," Harvey said to him.

Hawk gave him a wry smile. "Can't be any worse than getting around Aleppo with jihadis baying for your blood. I'll go. Finding that girl depends on it. I was curious about one other thing."

"What would that be?"

"The dead guy we brought in. He had a different tattoo on his arm."

"Several in fact," Anja replied. "We think that at some

stage in his life he was Russian Special Forces. Now working as a mercenary. Anything else?"

"No."

"Good," Anja said with a curt nod. "Go over the plan with Ilse. You will be in her hands."

"What do I get to do?" Jimmy asked, feeling left out.

"Find out which apartment he's in." Anja looked at her watch. "You've got ten hours. Find him."

The sat phone on the table beside Anja rang. She picked it up and looked at her team. "Get to work."

———

"THIS IS ANJA," she answered the call.

"How are things?" It was Thurston.

"Are you checking on me?" Anja asked curtly.

"No, I'm just asking how the team is getting along?"

Anja sighed. "I'm sorry. The team is fine, but..."

"But what?"

The Talon commander went on to tell her about the previous night's mission and the disaster unfolding in Mexico City. When she had finished, Thurston said, "Hell, if I tried to count up how many times Reaper had turned a place into a warzone I'd run out of fingers and toes. Trust your judgement and your instincts, Anja. That's why you're there. I've read your file, remember. You're good at what you do. What have you got planned next?"

"I'm sending Hawk into the middle of the warzone to find a person of interest who may have information that we need."

"Alone?"

"It is a case of one man is better than a team. Besides, he's assured me he can do it."

"It's your call. Good luck."

"Mary?"

"Yes?"

"I'm sorry—about before."

"Don't worry about it, Anja. I wouldn't expect anything else from one of my commanders if I was over-stepping. Keep me updated."

"Yes, ma'am."

The call disconnected and Anja stared at the hangar wall. She hated to second-guess herself, but hoped she was making the right decision.

———

"DOES the boss seem all right to you?" Hawk asked Ilse.

The intel officer cast a look over her shoulder. "She's fine. Maybe still finding her feet in some ways."

"Yeah, can't have been easy losing half her team."

"Not for any of us," Ilse replied.

Hawk suddenly remembered that his boss wasn't the only one to lose people that day. "I'm sorry, Ilse."

"Shall we get started?"

The Brit felt like a dick. "Yes."

She brought up a picture on the computer screen. "This is an aerial picture taken twenty minutes ago, covering the immediate area surrounding the apartment complex." She stabbed at the screen with her finger. "There are roadblocks here and here."

"Are they armed men manning them?"

"Yes, as far as we can tell. There may be a way in through this alley here or you can go over the top. The problem with that is you'll have to come down anyway to enter the apartment complex."

"All that could change between now and then," Hawk pointed out.

Ilse sighed. "It's fluid all right. You'll have to go with the best intel we have at the time."

Hawk stared at her skeptically.

"I promise you; it'll be good and up to date."

"How am I getting in and out?"

"The van." The screen zoomed out and the slender finger came into play again. "You'll leave it there and go in on foot."

"That's about six blocks," he pointed out.

"Seven actually."

"I'll need my runners on for that."

"I'll get you there. You just need to get yourself out."

———

"CHANGE OF PLANS, JAKE," Ilse's voice cut suddenly through his comms. "Hold where you are."

Hawk dropped to his knee in the shadows and pressed himself against the wall of a brick building. "What's up?"

"We've got more fires sprung up around the target building. You'll go in low. I'm just reconfiguring the route."

"Roger that."

While he waited, Hawk took time to triple-check his equipment. He was now decked out in body armor, ballistic helmet, and his webbing held extra ammunition for the suppressed Heckler & Koch MP5SD. On his thigh was the holstered SIG. He had Night Vision as well as flashbang grenades. After all, he was going into a war zone.

The sky above the neighborhood glowed orange from the multiple blazes. So far, his infiltration had gone to plan. He had to admit, Ilse knew her stuff. It was a pity that he'd not had her on some previous missions he'd gone dark on.

"Bravo One, Alpha Two, copy?"

Hawk pressed his transmit button. "Copy, Alpha Two."

"You've got a roadblock to the south and another

approximately three hundred meters to the east. Keep going straight on a hundred meters and turn north. Copy?"

"Roger, moving now."

Hawk came to his feet and moved forward cautiously until he reached the cross street. He paused and looked around the corner of the building to his right. About a hundred meters further along at another intersection he could see the roadblock. There were four shooters manning it. All of them looked to be wearing masks.

He waited a moment until he was sure they weren't looking his way before he crossed over.

Hawk continued along the street. Most of the housing blocks were darkened, however many of the streetlamps were still lit. Overhead a helicopter circled, its searchlight flickering across the buildings and streets below. In the distance the sound of automatic gunfire ebbed and flowed as some unseen battle raged.

"You're coming up to the street on your left, Jake," Ilse said in a low voice. "Take it."

He stopped at the intersection making sure it was clear. "Sounds like there's a party going on somewhere, Alpha Two. Got disco lights in the sky."

"Going by the chatter we're picking up, some cartel shooters have several police pinned down in an ambush."

Hawk traversed halfway along the street when Ilse came back to him. "Take the alley on your right, Jake. The next one over has a burning building on it. Also, there's a roadblock near the intersection to the north."

"Copy."

He could see the glow from the fire and the thick smoke it was sending skyward. The apartment block in front of it was illuminated and shadows danced across its orange façade.

Inside, the alley was darker, the building beside it blocking the false light. Garbage and 44-gallon drums littered the thoroughfare. Keeping his MP5 at his shoulder, Hawk walked towards the far end of the alleyway.

"Hold, Bravo One, hold!" The voice was urgent, demanding. Jake dropped to a knee behind one of the steel drums and waited.

At the mouth of the alley two armed men appeared. They stopped and began talking. Seconds dragged into minutes as it looked as though they had taken up station at the alley mouth. "That's inconvenient," Hawk muttered. "Fucking scousers."

"You'll have to go around, Jake," Ilse said.

"Screw that," he said quietly.

Hawk looked around him and found an empty bottle. He bent and picked it up. With his thumb he flicked the fire selector around to 3-round burst and rolled the glass bottle across the alley.

From where he was hidden, Hawk could hear the startled exclamation from one of the shooters. "What was that?"

"How should I know, go and have a look."

One of the men broke off from the other and walked into the darkened thoroughfare. From where he was hidden, Hawk watched him approach. Lowering the MP5, he retrieved his combat knife.

The shooter kept coming until he was level with Hawk's position. The Brit held his breath momentarily as his prey stopped and looked around. The man turned away and was about to call out to his friend when Hawk moved.

Springing up from his crouched position he clamped his left hand over the shooter's mouth. The man stiffened; his body ready to fight. However, the knife in Hawk's right hand rose and he buried it into the man's throat, withdrawing it quickly then reinserting it, this time forcing it forward so that the double-edged blade burst from the front of the man's throat in a spray of warm blood. The man's weapon fell to the alley's hard surface with a clatter.

As the shooter bled out Hawk dragged him behind the drums he'd been hiding behind. Hawk wiped the blade and sheathed it.

"Hey, Luis, where are you?" the second man called out, alerted by the noise of the gun falling to the ground.

When he wasn't answered, he tried again. "Luis? Answer me."

The man's curiosity at the silence drew him further into the alley. He was armed with a Kalashnikov of some descript. It was at his shoulder ready to fire, even at ghosts if need be.

Hawk waited until the man had moved his aimpoint to the left of his position before coming erect. The MP5 let forth a burst of fire, each round punching into the second shooter's chest.

The man never even cried out, just fell to the ground and remained still.

Hawk hurried forward and grabbed the dead man by the collar and pulled him deeper into the alley. With the body secure he walked towards the mouth of the alley. He pressed the transmit button on his comms and said, "Alpha Two, two X-Rays down, continuing mission."

"Copy, Bravo One."

At the alley mouth, Hawk stopped and scanned left and right looking for threats. To his right was another roadblock. This one closer than the last. The fire to his left was well ablaze, the building standing out like a giant beacon, illuminating the street and the target building to his front.

"Alpha Two, copy?"

"Copy, Bravo One."

"I've got a roadblock to the south. About fifty meters from my current location."

"Yes, I see it."

"You've put me right in their laps, Alpha Two." His voice was curt.

"Suck it up, Bravo One," came the response. "It was the only way in. Now, can you get across the street or, as you British say, take your bat and ball and go home? Over."

"I can see I'm going to like working with you more than I thought," he retorted.

"Is there an issue, Bravo One?" It was Anja.

"Negative, Alpha One."

"Then continue mission."

Hawk pulled a face, mimicking a nagging woman. "Yes, ma'am."

"I saw that, Bravo one."

Hawk looked directly above him and blew his commander a kiss.

"I saw that too."

The Brit watched the men on the checkpoint for a few minutes before readying himself. "Do we have a location yet?"

"Negative."

Thirty seconds later, Hawk ran across the street towards the building, praying that the men on the road-block wouldn't turn.

He slipped into the shadows and waited, getting his breathing under control. He edged along the building until he reached the corner of the main entrance. The apartments were a square U-shaped configuration with the carpark in the center. "Bravo One, going in."

"Copy, good luck."

Hawk started to move when his comms came alive again. "Jake? You there. It's Jedi Twenty-Four."

*What the fuck?* "Say again? Over."

"It's Jimmy."

"Jeez, kid, you really need to brush up on your radio protocols."

"Jimmy, get off this channel now," Anja snapped.

"I—I have something."

"What is it, Kid?" Hawk asked. "Make it quick."

"The person you're looking for is on the second floor. Apartment number twenty-four."

"Are you sure?"

"Yes."

"Roger that. Now get off the channel."

Hawk entered the complex and hurried to the stairs which led him to the second-floor landing that ran around the interior allowing access to the apartments. Upon reaching the landing he walked along it, counting off the numbers as he went until he reached the target unit.

There were two ways he could go in. Breach and bang or pick the lock and go with stealth. He chose the latter; maybe he should have gone with the first.

———

BULLETS ERUPTED through the paper-thin door in an explosion of razor-sharp splinters. The sound of the gunfire echoed around the courtyard tearing the night apart. Hawk hugged the wall cursing himself for not choosing his first option. Within the room, the gunfire stopped abruptly, and Hawk took a flashbang from his webbing and pulled the pin. Instead of having to open the door, he threw it through the melon-sized hole and ducked back. The explosion crashed from within and without hesitation, Hawk dropped his NVGs and entered.

The apartment wasn't big by any means. The door opened into the main room which comprised the kitchen and living room. The man he sought was staggering around trying to clear the effects of the grenade. In his hand was the weapon he'd been trying to reload.

By the time he realized he wasn't alone it was too late.

He straightened just in time to be greeted by Hawk's clenched fist.

With a grunt he dropped to the floor, the blow knocking him senseless. Hawk then checked the rest of the apartment, his practiced gaze looking for anything of importance.

On the dining table he saw a mess of scattered papers. He grabbed them and stuffed them inside his shirt. Once done he went back to the fallen man and knelt over him. He took out a small flashlight and slapped the downed Mexican across the face. "Come on, mate, wake up. It was just a fucking love tap."

The man moaned.

Hawk tried again. "Come on, mate, open those eyes."

Suddenly the man became more aware and lurched violently upward. Hawk hit him with a forearm and when he slumped back placed a knee in the middle of his chest."

"Calm down and answer some questions."

"Who are you?"

"Not important." Hawk ripped open the shirt and shone the flashlight onto the skin. There was the tattoo. "They own you, huh?"

"What are you talking about?"

"Medusa, cock. You know them. You and your mate were working for them."

"Bravo One, you've woken up the neighborhood. You have hostiles closing in on your position. Get out now."

"Shit." He rolled the Mexican onto his front and pulled his hands behind his back then cable tied them in place. He began to pull him to his feet. Looking down at the man's arm, he noticed something below the elbow. Hawk pulled up the sleeve to reveal a tattoo. Retrieving his cell from his pocket, he opened the camera function and took a picture. "Alpha Two, sending something your way."

"Roger."

"Come on, you, places to go."

Hawk pushed him towards the doorway. He let the MP5 hang from its strap and took out the SIG. Poking his head out the door, he scanned the vicinity to make sure it was clear. Growling to his prisoner, he said, "Give me any trouble and I'll put a frigging bullet in your head."

Guiding him along the landing, he stopped abruptly when firing erupted from down below. Bullets cracked as they flew past Hawk's head and hammered into the wall of the apartment behind him. The SIG in his fist came alive as Hawk returned fire at the shooter.

The man was joined by a second who cut loose with his own weapon. Debris rained all about the two men on the second-floor landing. Hawk ducked back from the railing. "Shit! Shit! Shit!"

He moved forward again and fired once more. Out of the five rounds that hammered out of the SIG's barrel, only one found its mark. The first shooter to arrive fell back with a bullet in his chest.

The second shooter ducked for cover giving Hawk time to get his prisoner moving. "Come on, asshole."

He shoved him along the landing towards the far end. More gunfire erupted and bullets chewed divots from the building's façade.

Hawk fired back as he moved, seeing another shooter fall. However, numerous others had joined in and things were starting to get hairy.

Suddenly a tattooed shooter appeared in front of him with a raised AK-47. Hawk cursed and shoved his prisoner aside. The SIG in his fist roared once more and the shooter fell.

"Screw this," the Brit snarled and put his SIG back in its holster, reaching for the MP5.

He brought it up and walked toward the rail. There were four targets below in the courtyard and he picked the closest one.

Hawk's finger caressed the trigger and a three-round burst spewed forth. The shooter jerked violently under the strikes and collapsed. The former SAS man shifted his aim and shot the next in line with another burst.

A hailstorm of lead forced Hawk to duck before he came back up. He flicked the fire selector to auto and cut loose with the rest of the magazine. The two shooters down below were torn to shreds by the barrage of bullets.

Hawk dropped out the magazine and replaced it with a fresh one. He turned to see his prisoner crouched in a doorway. The Brit grabbed his collar and dragged him to his feet. "Come on, mate, you're not dead yet."

He guided him towards the stairs, and they started down. Hawk pressed the transmit button on his comms and said, "Talk to me, Alpha Two."

"Jake, one of those X-Rays must have had a radio. You've got even more closing in on your position. I advise you to cut your prisoner free and get out."

"We still need him, Alpha Two," Hawk pointed out.

Anja came on the air. "It's your call, Jake. We'll guide you from here."

By the time they hit the courtyard the Brit had made his decision. "Continuing mission, Alpha Two."

"Copy, continuing mission." There was a pause in the transmission before Ilse came back on. "Jake, two X-Rays coming in from the front."

The MP5 snapped into line as they appeared. Jake had slipped the fire selector back to single shot and double-tapped them both. He and his prisoner kept moving forward. They exited the courtyard and walked onto the street.

"Bravo One, continue straight ahead into the alley. You've got X-Rays closing from both sides."

Hawk gave the Mexican a shove and he staggered forward. As they entered the alley he said, "Stop there."

The prisoner stopped.

"Sit down."

He didn't move.

Hawk stabbed a finger at him and said, "Sit the fuck down."

He sat.

"Jake, what are you doing?" Ilse asked, her normally calm voice showing a hint of urgency.

"Slowing them down."

"What?"

Ignoring her, he peered around the left side of the alley mouth. Coming along the street was a handful of armed men. He quickly glanced to the right and saw the other group converging on the first. "Let's see how you deal with this."

Hawk fired two bursts at the second group before turning and doing the same to the first. Suddenly the street came alive with automatic fire as the two clusters turned on each other thinking that they were being shot at by the opposite.

The Brit turned and hurried to his prisoner. Once more he dragged him to his feet and propelled him along ahead.

"Smart thinking, Bravo One," Ilse said over his comms.

"Best I could think of at the time."

Hawk and his prisoner reached the end of the alley. "Which way, Alpha Two?"

"Go right to the end of the street."

"Roger that."

"You will not get away, you know?" the man spoke for the first time since leaving the apartment block.

Hawk glared at him through the semi-dark. "Don't be too sure about that. I've been in worse shitholes than this one."

"They will stop you."

"Who? Medusa?"

"Uh, huh. Right now, they know what you are doing. Following your every move."

"What do you mean? How are they following my every move?"

"You think the tattoos are just tattoos? Think again, amigo."

Hawk slammed him against the wall. "What the fuck are you saying? Spit it out."

THWACK!

The Mexican's head seemed to explode before Hawk's eyes. Blood and brain matter sprayed across the wall behind him in some kind of sick psychedelic pattern.

The Brit swore vehemently and let him go to drop at the base of the structure. Hawk ran across the alley and took cover behind a garbage heap just as a second round came in, barely missing him.

"Alpha Two I've got a sniper somewhere and the HVT is down, KIA."

"Say again, Bravo One. Is the HVT KIA?"

"Affirmative. He's as dead as the dinosaurs, Alpha Two. I need you to pinpoint this fucking sniper for—"

WHACK!

The high-powered round buried itself in the garbage mound and burst through the other side. "Shit. Find the damned sniper, Ilse."

"Wait one."

"I don't have shitting one," Hawk snarled.

Another round came whistling in. The Brit hunkered down even lower.

Two more rounds, each one closer than the last.

"I have him, Bravo One. He's atop the building on the other side of the street. A third of the way along from the right side. Any idea who he is?"

"Same guy who took out the American in the club would be my guess."

"How would he know—"

"I don't know," Hawk said curtly. "I'll ask the frigging pillock when I talk to him."

Keeping low, Hawk edged around the garbage pile. He brought the MP5 up and sighted on where he figured the sniper was.

Another shot and he saw him. The round hammered into the stinking mess just before Hawk opened fire. He saw the bullet strikes and fired another burst. Before waiting to see the results, he was up and moving, fast. He burst from the alley mouth and dove behind a parked vehicle.

A bullet from the sniper punched into the rear quarter panel with a loud bang. Hawk came up and fired off the remainder of his magazine before reloading.

Two more high-powered rounds crashed into the vehicle. One of which smashed through the driver's side front window. Hawk came up and fired another burst. Then he was moving, sprinting across the street towards the building that the sniper was on top of. He reached the wall and pressed himself firmly against it.

"Sitrep, Bravo One," Anja asked.

"I've reached the building where the sniper is. I'm about to breach."

"Negative, Bravo One, RTB now."

She wanted him to break contact and return to base. "Ma'am—"

"Now, Jake. Something isn't right."

Hawk nodded. "All right, I'm RTB."

Then he slipped into the darkness with the help of Ilse and headed for his vehicle.

———

"SHIT!" Hawk grated as he slammed his hand upon the steering wheel of the SUV. He reached for his comms and said, "Alpha Two, copy?"

"I'm still here, Jake."

"Put everyone on level one alert, now."

"Jake, what—"

"Do it now and hook the boss in on the network."

A couple of moments later and Anja came back to him. "Is there something wrong, Jake?"

"The target said something to me before he died. He said I wouldn't get away. He asked me if I thought the tattoos were just tattoos. I don't think much of it but what if—"

"The tattoos have some kind of tracking isotope in them?" Ilse finished.

"That's how the snipers were able to home in on them."

"That's a long stretch," Anja said.

"Not if they had someone watching them already."

"You think they could have tracked the body we brought in, to our location?"

"I'd say there is a good chance."

There was muffled talk in the background and Anja said, "It looks like we're about to find out, Jake. Get back here now. Out."

# CHAPTER EIGHT

*The Hangar*

"GRIZZ, I've got movement near Outpost Two," Linc came over the net.

"What kind of movement?"

"Not sure, wait one."

"Mac, Nemo, you got anything?" Harvey asked his two other operators.

"All clear at Three, Grizz," Kent called in.

"Same at Four."

"Hey, Grizz?"

"Go, Linc."

"I've got maybe fifteen X-Rays pretending to be snakes in the grass over here."

"How far out, Linc?"

"About a hundred meters," Linc replied.

Harvey thought for a moment. It was a bad perimeter to defend and even when he set up the outposts he knew it would be all but impossible to do such a thing. "All right, Linc. Fall back to the Alamo. I'll call it in."

"Roger that."

"Mac, Nemo, you, too. Fall back."

"Roger that."

"Alpha Two this is Eagle One, over."

"Copy, Eagle One."

"We've got spooks inbound. We're falling back. Prepare for contact."

"Copy, Eagle One."

Harvey flicked the fire selector on his Bren2 around to auto and started toward the fortified position he and his men had set up when they'd arrived. It was time to go to work.

———

INSIDE THE HANGAR, Anja was shrugging into her body armor. Beside her Ilse was checking the chin strap on her ballistic helmet. Once it was done, she checked her NVGs to make sure they were working. Lastly, she picked up the MP5 off the table and looked at her boss. Anja glanced at her and nodded. There was no need for words; they knew what had to be done.

They started to walk towards the hangar doors when Jimmy called after them, "What about me?"

"Close the doors and lock them," Ilse called back. "Then turn out the lights and hide. Don't let anyone in here."

"What if someone comes in here?"

"Shoot them."

"All—all right."

Anja glanced at Ilse. "You know he's in more danger than they will be if he fires that thing, don't you?"

"I have no doubt."

Walking outside they found Harvey and the others at the defensive position he'd set up. "You ladies hunker down here with Mac. Nemo, get to your position."

"What about you and Linc?" Anja asked him.

"We'll be around, ma'am. We like to be on the move.

All right, NVGs down and laser sights on. Pick your targets, don't waste ammunition. Good luck."

The two operators disappeared into the darkness

They set up behind the sandbags which Harvey had organized. Mac's M249 was resting atop one of the bags. He looked at the two women beside him and asked, "You ladies been in a shit show before?"

"More than once," Anja commented.

"Good. Let's get some."

The flat crack of the suppressed sniper set up from Nemo started the ball. Suddenly the area seemed to fill with incoming attackers. Through the green of her NVGs Anja let the laser sight on the MP5 settle on a target before she squeezed the trigger. Beside her Ilse did the same and two attackers dropped mid-stride.

Mac opened fire with the SAW and the sound of casings hitting concrete tinkled in the night like a tinny windchime. His rounds mowed down a handful of men who died violently on the concrete apron.

Anja picked out another shooter and was about to fire when the ground to their left came alive. "Shit," she cried out dropping down for cover as a storm of fire came in. "On our left."

"Where did they come from?" Mac shouted. "Eagle One, we've got X-Rays in the wire from the east, over."

"Roger, Mac. On our—" The comms went dead.

"Say again, Grizz, over."

While Mac tried to regain contact with his commander, Ilse was crouched down changing out a spent magazine calmly like the seasoned vet that she was. Once the weapon was ready, she came back up and let loose with a long burst of automatic fire at the newcomers.

An explosion ripped through the air just short of their position. A giant fireball leaped into the air, illuminating the night. Ilse ducked down and hissed as her NVGs flared. She lifted them and prepared to fire once more. She rose once more and through the orange glow picked out a target. The MP5 rattled and bullets kicked up debris behind the running man.

"Fuck it," she growled and fired again. Albeit too late.

"Grizz, are you there, damn it?" Mac asked, still trying to get through.

"I'm here, Mac," Harvey replied, and on the flank of the attackers two weapons opened and drove the eastern assault back.

The glow of the fire had died down and Ilse dropped her NVGs back into place. An eerie silence settled over the field. Out of the darkness Linc and Harvey appeared. "Everyone all right?" the big man asked.

"I think so," Anja replied. "How about you, Mister Harvey?"

"We're good, ma'am. I can say this, working for you certainly isn't dull."

"I could take dull."

The big man chuckled. "Nemo, talk to me."

"They've pulled back, Grizz. I think they're regrouping."

"Roger that."

Harvey unhooked two fragmentation grenades from his webbing and sat them on the sandbags near Anja. "They're there if you need them, ma'am."

She nodded. "Let's hope I don't."

"Where the hell are they coming from is what I want to know?" Linc growled. "Someone who can pull together a small army like that on short notice—"

His words were cut short by Nemo. "Here they come again. From the west this time. Shit, there's even more of them."

The sound of automatic fire tore the night apart and once more the darkness was filled with incoming rounds. Anja dropped lower so the sandbags would cover most of her body, leaving only her head and shoulders exposed.

Her finger depressed the trigger on the MP5 at the sight of the new assault coming in. After four rounds being fired the weapon fell silent and she cursed herself for not reloading while she had the chance.

Anja changed the magazine for a fresh one and by the time she was ready to fire it seemed as though the attackers had closed in on the defenders.

"Son of a bitch," Mac shouted from beside her. "These pricks are fucking military."

"What?" Anja snapped.

"Mexican military."

"I heard that. What—"

Her question was never spoken for at that moment a vehicle with a heavy caliber machine gun fixed to it roared into sight to join the fray.

"Shit!" Mac growled and shifted his aim with the SAW. He depressed the trigger and burned though half of his belt of ammunition. He reached for his comms and pressed the transmit button. "Nemo, get that fucking gunner."

Bullets sparked off the vehicle, but it still came on. The heavy machine gun chugged out rounds which had the capability of ripping off limbs.

Anja's magazine ran dry but instead of reloading, she grabbed at a grenade on the sandbag. Pulling the pin, she threw it as far as she could. *"Frag out!"*

The airfield was rocked by another explosion. This one however lifted the front of the armored vehicle as it was engulfed in flame. The machine crashed back down, the shooter in the back falling to the concrete apron, burning like a Roman candle.

"Top throw, ma'am," Mac shouted above the din as Anja reloaded her MP5.

Beside her, Ilse picked out a target and fired twice. Her target went down but she felt a burning sensation bite into her upper left arm. She glanced at it and noticed the tear in her shirt. She'd been hit but not badly.

Mac grunted and cursed out loud before sliding to the ground behind the sandbags. Ilse glanced at him and saw him lying there. "Man down!"

She hurried to his side. Anja kept firing. "Check him out."

The Talon commander fired until her next magazine was dry before she pressed her comms button. "Eagle One we've got a man down."

"On my way."

Anja looked up to notice more attackers coming their way. She let the MP5 fall and lunged for the SAW. Sighting on the closest assailant she squeezed the trigger and felt the staccato hammering at her shoulder.

The man she'd aimed at went down flailing. She shifted the sights and fired a longer burst which saw two more fall. Suddenly Harvey appeared beside her, his Bren2 hammering methodically. Beside him, Linc joined them. "Ilse, sitrep on Mac?"

"He's still alive but I'm not sure how hard he's been hit."

"Get me up and I'll show you," the wounded man grated.

"Stay there," Linc snapped. "We've got this."

Moments later, the firing died down and finally stopped altogether. Harvey reloaded his weapon and looked down at Ilse who was still working on Mac. "Linc, give her a hand."

They looked around their immediate vicinity, illuminated by the burning vehicle. There were bodies everywhere. Anja shook her head. "We have to get out of here."

"Yes, ma'am."

The screech of tires broke through their trances as the van appeared rocketing across the apron. Hawk brought the vehicle to a sudden stop and leaped from the driver's seat. "Looks like you lot have been having a party without me."

"Something like that," Harvey said, rolling his eyes.

"Everyone all right?"

"Nothing we can't handle."

Hawk frowned and walked across to one of the fallen men. "Hey, you know these guys are Mexican military, right?"

"Someone did mention that," Anja replied.

"This is bad."

"Yes, it is. Very bad."

Hawk looked around. "So much for surgical strike team."

# CHAPTER NINE

*The Hangar*

"ILSE, I need you to check this for me," Hawk said holding out a piece of paper.

She looked at him. "I don't have time, Jake. We're packing up, remember?"

"I think it's important. Just a couple minutes."

Frustrated, she snatched it from his hand. Maybe a little too forcefully but at that moment she didn't care. She stared at it and said, "It looks like a cargo manifest."

"Yes, it does."

She shoved it back at him. "There, I looked at it."

Hawk wouldn't be perturbed. "Did you see what the manifest was for?"

"No, I didn't."

"It's for dolls."

Ilse looked at him. "So? Look, Jake, take this to the point. We need to get done."

"I took it from the apartment where the Mexican lived. Why would he have a cargo manifest for dolls?"

Ilse stopped what she was doing and snatched the

paper back. "Because they weren't shipping dolls. They were shipping people."

"My thoughts exactly."

"All right," the intel officer said waving at her equipment. "You get this on the plane, and I'll have a look at this."

"Thanks."

"Don't thank me yet, it may be nothing."

———

"COME WITH ME," Ilse said to Hawk five minutes later. He followed her to her destination. Anja Meyer. "Miss Meyer, Jake has found something I think needs following up."

"What is it, Ilse? We don't have time. We need to be wheels up. Mac is stable but he needs care."

"I know, but he found this manifest for dolls, in the apartment. I looked into the company, and they have a fleet of cargo aircraft. Jake and I think that the dolls were actually women."

"Where did the shipment go?"

"I don't know. There is a number but nothing else."

"What about hacking their computer system? Is there a way in?"

"I tried in the limited time I had but there was nothing about a shipment of dolls. I think the only way to find out is to get into their office and have a look for a hardcopy. If they're doing what we think they are, then they won't keep it electronic. Or if it is, it won't be able to be remote accessed."

"Where is their office located?"

"Mexico City."

"Damn it. What else do we have?"

"That's all."

"I can get in there, ma'am," Hawk said. "I just need the opportunity."

"But we're leaving."

"Then leave. I'll stay and get the information that we need."

Anja stared at him. "All right I'll make a call. But know this, Jake, you'll be on your own. If you get into trouble, I can't help you."

Hawk nodded. "It's all right, ma'am. I think I know someone who can help."

––––––––

"JAKE! How are they hanging, old mate?" came the heavy British accent of a thin man with straggly hair.

"I need your help, Barney," Hawk said as he entered the apartment.

"Come on in and tell me what I can do," Barney Walsh said to his former colleague from the service. "How long has it been? The Congo?"

"Something like that, Barney. You look like shit."

"Yeah, well, it's been a while. What are you doing in Mexico City at a time like this?"

"On a job."

"Doing what?"

"Need to know, Barney."

"Of course, it is."

"Can you help me to get into the offices of Rotor Transport?" Hawk asked his former colleague.

Barney held his arms out from his side. "Look at me, Jake. Do I look like I can help you?"

Hawk shook his head. The man was far from the operator he'd known in the Congo. "I got no one else, Barney. It's work five large."

"US or UK?"

"US."

Barney licked his lips. "What do you need me to do?"

"Just help me get into the place so I can have a look around and get out. That's all. Nothing we haven't done before."

"I'm not the man I was before, Jake. But all right, I'll help."

Hawk retrieved an envelope from his back pocket and removed half the promised money and dropped it onto a coffee table cluttered with empty bottles and cans. "What the fuck happened, Barney?"

"I—I lost my nerve, Jake. Just couldn't go do it no more. So I came here to Mexico—"

"To get away from it," Hawk finished. "Instead of getting your head right."

"It's not that simple, Jake. If it was, I'd still be in the Regiment."

"What about your wife and kid, Barney?" Jake asked. "What happened to them?"

"The cow left me when I started hitting the booze. Don't blame her, but she wouldn't let me see Billy."

There was a rattle at the door, the sound of keys. Hawk's hand blurred and his SIG appeared from inside his pants. Barney's hand shot out. "Easy, Jake. Fuck, put it away before Teresa sees it."

"I'm home, Barney," a woman's voice called. "And you'd better be sober, asshole."

Hawk put the gun away before the woman appeared. When she walked into the living room she stopped and stared at Hawk. "Who are you? Who is this, Barney?"

Teresa had long dark hair and was athletically built. She was pretty in her own way with two teardrop tattoos on her left cheek and gang tattoos on her arms. "This is a friend of mine from my Regiment days, Teresa? His name is Jake."

"What does he want?" she asked suspiciously.

"He came by to give me some money."

"What for?"

"He—"

"I was repaying a debt," Hawk said, cutting him off.

"He better not be some kind of fucking law, Barney. Roberto will skin you alive."

"Who's Roberto?" Hawk asked.

"He is my brother," Teresa shot back.

"I can promise you, Teresa, I'm not the law. I'm just here on holiday."

"Whatever."

She turned and walked out of the room. Hawk glared at Barney. "What the fuck, Barney?" he whispered harshly. "Who is Roberto?"

"Her brother, like she said."

"What does he do, Barney?"

"This and that."

"Don't shit me, Barney, those were gang tattoos she had on her, not nightclub fucking stamps."

"All right. He might have something to do with Los Demonios de la Muerte."

"The Devils of Death?" Hawk couldn't believe what he was hearing. "What is he, Barney? A foot soldier? Sicario? What?"

"He might be the boss?"

"Fuck me."

"It's not that bad, Jake. Really it isn't."

Hawk bent down to pick up the envelope of money. "Forget about it, Barney. I'm leaving."

The former Regiment man grabbed Hawk by the arm. "Wait, Jake. Don't go. Let me help you."

Hawk looked at the hand holding onto him and then saw the track marks in his friend's arm. Suddenly he realized his mistake. He pulled his arm from Barney's grasp and said, "Sorry, Barney. Be seeing you around."

"Come on, Jake," Barney called after him. "Wait, man. I can help you."

But the door closed behind Hawk and the Talon operative left.

———

ELEVEN HOURS LATER, Hawk stood across the street in the shadows of a doorway studying the office block before him. The only lights on were the security ones and those in the foyer where the security guards were stationed. From what he could make out, there were three of them.

So, he waited. The next thirty minutes dragged on interminably until finally two of them stood up and adjusted their jackets and pants, then moved off on patrol, leaving the single guard at the station in the foyer. When the man was alone, Hawk made his move.

He ran across the street and approached the main entrance. The guard looked up from behind the console and saw Hawk approaching at a run. When the Talon agent reached the entry, he started banging on the door and shouting. "Let me in, man. They're after me. Let me in."

"Go away," the guard shouted back.

"Let me in, they'll kill me."

"Who will?"

"The guys, they're coming after me. Let me in will you?"

The guard hesitated and reached for his radio mic. He said something and then walked towards the door. Using his key, he unlocked the door and let Hawk in.

"Thanks, man, you saved my skin."

"Who are you?"

"Big."

"Big?"

"Yeah, big fucking mistake," Hawk growled, and his right hand shot out and hit the guard in the throat. The man went to his knees, gasping, trying to breathe. "Take it easy, you'll be right."

Hawk hit him again. This time with the butt of the SIG. The guard went limp, and the Brit dragged him by his collar across the floor, placing the body behind the console out of sight.

From the console, Hawk made his way to the elevators. Ilse had told him that the director's office was on the top floor of the three-floor building. The elevator dinged and the doors opened. He walked in and pressed the appropriate button. As the elevator climbed towards its destination, Hawk drew the SIG and stepped to one side.

The conveyance slowed and then stopped with its telltale jolt. The doors slid open, and Hawk swept left and right with his weapon. It was clear.

Set out in an open plan type configuration, the floor had small cubicles where each employee worked. Towards the rear was the main office. Hawk walked swiftly through the maze of cubicles until he reached the door. Trying the handle, he found it locked. He couldn't be that lucky. Stepping back, the Brit raised his booted foot and kicked the door hard. Wood splintered as it flew back. No sense in taking the gentle route; he was on the clock.

Hawk crossed the threshold and walked over to the desk. Trying the drawers, he found they were like the door. It only took a few heartbeats to adjust them.

He flicked through the contents of each drawer, not finding what he was looking for. He glanced at the computer on the desktop and dismissed it. Ilse was right, anything important wouldn't be electronically accessible.

That left the filing cabinet.

Crossing from the desk to the back wall, he looked around briefly to make sure his presence was still undetected, before trying the top drawer. Of course, it was locked. He reached for the knife tucked behind his back beside the SIG. Removing it, it took only a few moments before he managed to jimmy the lock.

He began shuffling through the files inside then stopped. Where was it that crooks always kept their secret stuff? In the back. His hand found it right away. "You have to love the movies," he muttered.

Hawk flicked through the book and discovered it was some kind of ledger. It wasn't clear what for exactly but he figured that to be hidden away like it was, it had to be important.

Suddenly the screech of tires from outside caught his ear. He walked across to the large window and looked down. He saw five vehicles with armed men pouring from them. But only one caught his eye.

"Shit, Barney."

"Hold it, there," a voice said from behind Hawk.

"You took your time," Hawk said without facing him.

"Turn around."

"You might want to look out the window, mate. You've got some visitors."

"Turn around, puta."

The sound of gunfire rattled from down below. "See, told you."

The man worked his way around the Brit and looked out the window. "Fuck."

Hawk looked at him. This guy was far from Latino. "My guess is they're on their way up here. I managed a rough count and I think there's about fifteen of them."

"Who are they?" There was an accent. European.

"Ever heard of a group of scousers called Los Demonios de la Muerte?"

"Shit," the man hissed and reached into his pocket. He wasn't worried about Hawk anymore.

"What are you doing?"

"Calling for help."

"Mate, these bastards are already here. Help might as

well be in Brighton. But if we work together, we might get out of this alive."

"What are you thinking?"

"What's your name?"

"Nicolai."

"You had any training, Nicolai?"

"Yes."

"All right, then you know what we have to do. How do we get out of here?"

"The roof and across to the next building?"

"No back stairs?" Hawk asked hopefully.

Nicolai shook his head. "No."

"Of course not. Lead the way, Vlad."

"My name is Nicolai," the guard said correcting him.

"Just fucking move."

Hawk tucked the ledger inside his shirt and followed him out the office door. They started to make their way through the cubicles when two shooters appeared at the far end of the floor and opened fire without warning.

"Shit a brick," Hawk growled, throwing himself to the floor. Nicolai did the same as bullets tore through the flimsy thin cubicle dividers.

The Brit rose and fire a handful of shots at the shooters. Nicolai followed suit but they were forced low after two more appeared. "Where to?" Hawk shouted at Nicolai."

The guard lay on his back and pointed towards the far corner of the room. "That way."

Hawk ground his teeth together and said, "If you get me killed, Vlad, I'm going to be pissed."

"Me? I'm not the one they're after."

*You're right there.*

Keeping low, Hawk moved, dodging through the vacant cubicles as dust and debris rained down. "This is so not fucking good, Jake."

Suddenly he stopped. He could see the door—and the

fifteen feet between cover and the way out. He looked back at Nicolai. "What's this shit?"

The guard shrugged.

Hawk rose above the nearest cubicle and fired three rounds at a shooter. The man cried out and fell from sight. The Brit shifted his aim and fired again, another gangster fell, bringing forth a furious storm of gunfire.

Not long after it reached its peak, the gunfire stopped. Hawk looked confusedly at Nicolai. A voice called out. "Gringo? Are you still alive?"

Hawk said nothing.

"I know you have money, Gringo. A lot of money."

*Fucking Barney.* "Someone lied to you, mate. I've not got two coins to rub together between my ass cheeks."

"You lie, amigo. Your friend, he say so."

Hawk's expression grew hard. "He's not my friend."

"Come on, Jake, just hand the money over and we'll go. Roberto said so," Barney called out.

"Screw you, Barney, you prick. If I get a chance, I'm going to put a bullet in your dope addled brain."

"Don't be like that, Jake. You don't know me—what it's been like."

"Amigo," Roberto called to him. "Give us the money and we'll be gone."

Hawk looked at Nicolai. The guard shook his head. "They will kill us anyway."

"I kind of figured that."

"Well, amigo?"

"I told you, Pancho, I don't have any money."

"That is so sad," Roberto replied. There was a scuffle and a loud protest before the Mexican gangster said, "I will kill your friend if you do not hand it over."

"Wait, Roberto, what are you doing?"

Hawk could tell by the tone in Barney's voice that something wasn't right. "Wait, I'm going to stand up."

"No, don't," Nicolai said.

Hawk came to his feet and stood erect. Roberto had a gun pointed at Barney's head. The Talon agent shook his head. "You're a fucking scouser, Barney."

"I'm sorry, Jake."

"Screw you."

"Shoot him, Roberto."

It was a set up.

The gun in Roberto's hand blurred with movement and before Hawk could move, the weapon had been fired. The bullet hammered into Hawk's chest and knocked him back, arms flailing until he hit the floor.

It felt as though he'd been kicked by a horse, all the air rushing from his lungs as he gasped like a fish out of water. Near him, Nicolai came to his feet and fired his sidearm. Half a magazine exploded across the room finding soft flesh.

On the floor, Hawk moaned and looked down to where he'd been shot. He could see the hole in his shirt but no blood. Then he realized, the ledger.

With a shaking hand he pulled it clear of his shirt. There, in the center of the cover, was a hole. Luckily, however, the round hadn't passed through. "Holy shit."

Nicolai dropped beside him. "Are you alright?"

"Apart from being kicked by a horse I'm good."

"We need to get out the door."

"No shit."

"I'll go first. Cover me."

Hawk climbed to his knees while Nicolai poised himself to go. The Brit grabbed his arm. "Don't get shot."

Hawk came up and fired off what was left in his magazine. He saw three men fall and shifted his aim when he saw Barney. "Got you, you prick."

He squeezed the trigger, but nothing happened. "Bloody hell."

Dropping down, he began to reload, looking across in time to see Nicolai hit the door with his shoulder.

The door crashed back as the guard disappeared through it.

Hawk smashed the magazine home in anger before picking up the ledger and putting it back inside his shirt. Then he came to his feet and ran.

———

HAWK DOVE headlong through the open doorway and skidded to a stop at the foot of the stairs. He came to his feet and gathered himself. Nicolai looked over his shoulder from where he was shooting. "Up! Go up!"

Hawk started up the stairs, taking them two at a time. Behind him he could hear Nicolai. "The door will be locked. You need to hit it hard."

The Brit never even broke stride when he reached the door. Dropping his shoulder, he crashed into the door dead center.

The door flew back, and Hawk stumbled through. He fell to the roof and felt the skin come off his knuckles. Rolling, he came to his feet and looked around. The rooftop was covered in cooling towers for the air inside.

"This way," Nicolai snapped as he ran past the Brit.

Hawk followed him but they hadn't gone far before the shooting commenced once more.

They took cover behind one of the towers, the bullets clanging as they hit the metal casing of them. Nicolai changed his magazine and said, "Can you jump?"

"Why?"

"To the next building."

"How far?" Hawk asked, startled at the prospect.

"About twelve feet."

"You're shitting me," he groaned. "First I get shot and now you expect me to jump the English fucking Channel."

"You can go back the other way if you want."

"It might be safer."

"Are you ready?"

"No."

"See you over there."

Nicolai came to his feet and started running toward the edge of the building. Hawk shook his head and mumbled, "This is a bad idea."

Then he was up and moving, lead hornets chasing him all the way. As he closed on the edge of the yawning gap between the two structures, he actually thought he was going to make it. He was wrong.

At the last moment Hawk faltered and fell short. He cried out in pain as he hit the wall of the building like one of the characters in a Looney Tunes cartoon. He bounced back off the wall and fell the thirty odd feet toward the alley below. "Motherfu—"

———

IT'S amazing how much a pile of garbage will break your fall. Won't do much for your smell, but stopping you from dying, it is invaluable.

Hawk gathered himself and rolled from the stinking heap. He gagged at the fetid smell and came to his feet. Looking up to gauge how far he'd fallen, he shook his head and whistled. "A man doesn't go that far on vacation."

He started along the alley when gunfire hammered down from above. Hawk whirled and brought up his SIG. It blasted four times and a figure toppled from the rooftop, hitting the pavement with a sickening thud. "Bet that hurt."

Hawk turned and ran from the alley, bullets chasing him as he went. As he emerged from the narrow thorough-fare, he sighted the vehicles the gangsters had arrived in. He started toward them until he sighted two men: both armed, both gangsters. Hawk's SIG came up and fired twice. Both men dropped.

Hawk then shot out one of the tires on each vehicle before he vanished into the darkness. Moments later, the gangsters appeared on the street, led by Roberto. The angry gang leader began waving his arms in the air as he directed his people to go in different directions. The gesture was futile, Hawk was gone.

———

"NOT SO FAST, MY FRIEND," Nicolai said from the darkness.

Hawk turned slowly from the van's driver-side door. The guard emerged from the shadows into the moonlight, his boot crunching on the glass from the overhead street-lamp that Hawk had busted when he'd first arrived on station. "I see you made it."

Nicolai nodded. "As did you. Lucky, huh."

"Very. That fall was a potential killer."

"I want the book."

"The book?"

"The one you stole from the office."

Hawk shook his head. "I need it."

"So do I."

"Do you know what's in it?" Hawk asked.

"I do."

"Then you know why I need it. I'm looking for a girl."

"There's been a few."

"Fair hair, good looking, name of Maya."

"They never kept them onsite. The others looked after them."

"You mean the ones who are dead?"

"Dead?"

"Yeah, we found two of them. A Mexican and a Russian. Like you, I'm guessing. They were shot by a sniper."

Nicolai shifted uncomfortably. "Dead?"

"That's what I said. You see, we figured that the tattoos they were wearing had some kind of isotope in them which made them trackable." The Russian scratched at his chest. "You got one too, huh? After tonight I guess your days are numbered too."

"Not if I take the book back."

"Tell me what I want to know, and I'll give you the book."

Nicolai shook his head. "No. I cannot."

"Don't make me kill you, Nicolai," Hawk said. "Just make the trade."

"No." -

"Shit."

Both weapons came up like in some long forgotten western movie when two quick-draw artists went at it to see who was fastest. The gun in Hawk's fist crashed, the recoil pulsing up his arm. The bullet from the SIG punched into Nicolai's chest, driving him back. The Brit shot him again and the Russian fell.

"Stubborn bastard," Hawk growled. He took out his cell and took a photo of the dead man before climbing into the van and driving away.

# CHAPTER TEN

---

*Brownsville, Texas*

"YOU STINK," Anja said to Hawk. "Go and get cleaned up."

"Nice to see you too," he replied with a grin.

"The showers are through there," his boss said, pointing towards a doorway. "Come back when you're less smelly."

"Yes, ma'am."

"What's that you have?" Ilse asked curiously, indicating the ledger.

"I'm hoping information." He passed it to her and the first thing she noticed was the bullet hole. "What happened here?"

Hawk started walking towards the shower room. "I got shot."

"What?" She started following him and before she knew it she was in the shower room.

"Saved my life that ledger did," he said as he took his shirt off.

Ilse noticed the purple bruise on his chest. Without

thinking, she stepped forward and touched the area lightly. "Does it hurt?" she asked and looked up into Hawk's face suddenly realizing just how uncomfortably close she was.

Their eyes remained locked for a moment before Hawk said, "Not so much now."

Ilse stepped back and noticed the other bruises sketched across his torso and arms. "Where did the others come from?"

"Them? I fell off a building." He waved his hand as though it was an everyday occurrence and was no big deal.

Now she was stunned. "You fell—how did you fall?"

"We had some dickheads shooting at us and I tried to jump a gap between buildings. Needless to say that I didn't quite make it."

"We?"

"Yeah, a Russian tosser and me."

"How does he fit into this?"

"Is this some kind of debrief?" Hawk asked.

"Not really."

Hawk dropped his pants and Ilse turned away, her face reddening. "Good, because if you hadn't noticed, I stink like a sewer."

She nodded. "Sorry."

"Unless you want to scrub my back?"

"I'll wait for you to finish."

Twenty minutes later, he was seated at a table with Anja, Ilse, and Harvey, giving them the rundown on everything that had happened.

"You were sure lucky," Harvey stated.

"I just hope it was worth it." He rubbed his hand through his hair and gave a tired grin.

Ilse nodded. "It would seem that Medusa has been sending the girls they grab from Mexico, out to Brazil and Europe. It's a happy hunting ground for them because of the quantity of American girls who come across the border for a weekend of partying."

"Is there anything in there about Maya?" Hawk asked.

"Not exactly. There is, however, mention of a shipment of dolls—"

"How many?" Hawk interrupted.

"Four."

"To where?"

"Brazil."

"So that's where they've taken her."

"That would be my guess."

Hawk looked at Anja. "What now, Boss?"

"I have a contact in Brazil. I'll reach out and see if something can be organized for us." She rose immediately, eyeing them momentarily before retrieving her encrypted cell from her pocket. Then she walked away from the group.

"You look like shit," Harvey said.

"I've felt better. I think I shook something up when I fell off that building."

"Fell?" the American asked with raised eyebrows.

"All right, jumped."

"Take your shirt off, Jake," Ilse ordered him.

Hawk pretended to give her an embarrassed look. "But, Ilse, we're in company. Can't you wait until we are in private?"

"Cut the crap and just do it," she said getting out of her seat. "Stand up."

Jake did as she asked, and Ilse could see that the bruises were somewhat more pronounced than when she first saw them. She gently poked and prodded at each with her fingers. When she reached the one on his back, Hawk took in a sharp breath. "That hurts."

"You could have a cracked rib, Jake. I'll tape you up and you'll need to take it easy for a few days."

"I don't have time to take it easy."

"Orders, Jake."

Hawk raised his eyebrows. "You outrank me?"

"Yes, I do."

"Shit. All right, if you insist."

Ilse smiled, exposing a straight row of white teeth. "I do. We'll do it after the briefing."

He replaced his shirt and sat back down. A few minutes later, Anja reappeared. "All right, we leave for Brazil tomorrow."

"What about Mac, ma'am?" Harvey asked.

"He'll remain behind until he's fit enough to catch us up. You can work one man down?"

"Yes, ma'am."

"Jake is out of action for a couple of days as well," Ilse informed her boss.

"Why?"

"Ribs. I checked him over and he may have a cracked or broken one in there somewhere."

"He has until we get to Brazil, I need him in the field."

"Yes, ma'am."

Ilse looked at Hawk who was grinning. She poked her tongue out at him and grinned back. Anja said, "Make sure all our equipment is ready to go. Wheels up at oh-six-thirty.

---

*Over the Caribbean Sea*

Hawk sat with Anja and Ilse as they went over the file containing everything they knew. Ilse and Jimmy had been working nonstop gathering all they could in preparation for the next phase of the operation. Anja said, "My contact in Brazil said that their taskforce has been aware of the trafficking ring for a while now. However, each time they try to do something about it, their operation is either blown or canceled."

"Why canceled?" Hawk asked.

"He says that there is interference from higher up the chain."

"You have to love corruption," Hawk said sarcastically.

"When we land, we'll link up with their taskforce. They'll take us to their base of operations, and we'll work from there."

"What's your contact's name?"

"His name is Elias, that's all I'm prepared to tell you. Our being there is unsanctioned, and it could land him in trouble if we are found out."

"Yes, ma'am."

Ilse cleared her throat and said, "Jimmy and I did a deep search on your man Nicolai. He too was scrubbed like the others, but someone didn't use enough bleach to make him disappear completely."

She opened a folder and took out two pictures, passing them to Anja and Hawk. "Nicolai Kamenev. Former Russian army. Reported killed in action in Syria two years ago. That got me thinking. I ran another check on your guy from the nightclub. Leo Sorokin, also Russian army, reported killed in Chechnya last year on a terrorist operation."

"So, are we all thinking that this whole thing is a Russian operation?" Hawk asked.

"It would seem that way. But whoever is behind it, they are extremely skilled at what they do."

Hawk glanced at Anja who seemed to have a worried expression on her face. "Ma'am, are you alright?"

"What? Yes—yes I'm fine."

"It might not be," Ilse said reading her mind.

"It's too much of a coincidence, don't you think?"

"What is?" Hawk asked, looking from one woman to the other.

Anja sighed. "Viktor Medvedev."

"*The* Viktor Medvedev?"

"Yes."

"Are you sure?"

Anja nodded.

Hawk stared at Ilse and said, "You'd better read me in."

A few minutes later, Ilse had a picture of the man. She passed it to Hawk and said, "Viktor Medvedev. Early forties, former Russian FSB. Left after he found he could make more money by selling guns and flesh. Makes Viktor Bout look like a schoolboy."

The former SAS man nodded. He'd heard of Bout. He was also known as the Merchant of Death. Had sold arms across the globe until he was taken off the board and locked away in an American prison.

"We had solid intel that two terror cells were in Berlin. Problem being that unbeknown to us, that intel was fed to us by him. It was revenge for a deal we had spoiled the previous year. Fifty million it was worth. We put Valkyrie into action and had our team in the field."

Anja took up the story. "I ordered the team to breach, but the target was rigged with explosives. The entire assault team was wiped out."

"Shit," Hawk muttered.

"That wasn't all. Just before the attack went in, we thought there was trouble with the comms. We couldn't reach the field agents who were onsite. When we finally worked out there was something wrong, it was too late. Then as if to rub salt into the wound, he detonated a bomb in the center of the city. I made myself a promise that day. I would kill him no matter what or how long it took. Now it looks as if I might get that chance."

"You can't make this personal, ma'am," Hawk said.

"I can make it whatever I want to," she shot back at him, fixing him with a withering look.

"Hey, I'm all for giving this bloke what he deserves, but you have to be wise about it or be prepared to lose another team."

Anja's glaring look began to soften. "You're right."

"Let's get this girl and then go after him. Providing that it is him behind Medusa."

"It's him," Anja said grimly. "I know it."

———

Victor Medvedev leered openly at the two young Sudanese women standing naked before him. He marveled at their almost flawless forms. So athletic yet so —the door opened and interrupted his thoughts. He turned his angry glare at the man who had just entered. "What is it, Leonid?" he snapped.

"There has been an issue in Mexico which appears about to spill over in Brazil."

Medvedev held his withering stare on the thin man for several moments before breaking off and turning to speak with the handler who'd brought the women in. "Take them back to the cells for transportation. Ensure they are tattooed before they leave."

As the party of three disappeared, the Russian dealer turned his hot gaze on Leonid. "How many times do you have to be told, Leonid?"

"It is important, sir," the man implored him.

"It always is. All right, tell me what is so *important*."

"We have been forced to liquidate our operation in Mexico. Everyone involved has been removed from the equation."

"Everyone? What do you mean everyone?"

"The pickup team, those involved in shipping; the government officials that were bribed; everyone. There was no other option but to have the security team neutralize them all."

Anger surged through the Russian. "You'd better tell me everything, Leonid."

For the next ten minutes, Leonid told Medvedev of the catastrophe that had befallen their operation in Mexico. "Do we know who these people are?"

Leonid shook his head. "All that we can be sure about is that they are well-trained."

"How did they discover our operation?"

"From what I understand they are looking for an American girl picked up by the team."

"Where is she now?"

"Brazil."

"Do you know where they are now?"

"No, sir."

Medvedev nodded slowly. "Find them. They are a threat that needs to be neutralized. Assemble a team for the job. Where is Kir? His team would be the best."

"They are in Mali."

"Bring them back. Take care of it; I have a meeting in Dubai. I leave within the hour."

"Yes, sir."

———

*Mali*

The sound was mournful. It was one of wailing despair by those that remained of the once happy village. Dead and dying lay all around the big blond Russian, even at his feet. Rich, dark blood soaked the Mali soil while the scent of smoke and burning flesh was carried on the light breeze.

Kir Rogov turned to the man nearest him, indicated to the small group of young women and asked, "Is that all of them, Fedor?"

Fedor Varkov was a tall man, yet not as broad in shoulder as his team commander. "It is, sir."

"Fifteen?"

"Yes."

"It'll have to do. Get them ready to travel."

"Yes, sir."

"What do we do with the rest, Kir?"

Rogov turned to the woman beside him. She was armed with an AK-74, wore full body armor, and looked like she was born to the life of a mercenary. Her dark hair was cut short, tucked under a New York Yankees ball cap.

"Get rid of them, Luba. Make sure it looks like the Mali Front were responsible."

The Mali Front were extremists who had risen to fame over the past two years through acts of violence in their efforts to overthrow the government. Villages had been destroyed, hundreds kidnapped, and many more murdered in their campaign of terror which rivaled that of Boko Haram.

Rogov's team had been in Africa for the past three weeks gathering women to fulfil 'orders'. This village was to be their last in Mali before leaving to head for Libya.

"Boss, a call," another mercenary called out waving an encrypted satellite phone.

"Who is it?" he asked irritated.

"Leonid."

"What does that prick want?"

"I don't know, ask him."

Rogov took the phone and grunted. "What?"

"This prick wants you to get your ass on a plane. I have a job for you."

"I already have one."

"Just do it, Kir, before I have you replaced by someone who is more pliable."

"You mean someone who will take your shit," Kir

snapped. He and Leonid had never seen eye to eye and their animosity toward each other was always apparent.

"Just do it, you horse's ass."

"Yes, sir. What about my latest acquisitions?"

"Get rid of them."

The call disconnected and Rogov turned to Luba Zolotova. "Change of plans. Kill them all."

# CHAPTER ELEVEN

*Brazil*

A SMALL, armored convoy sped through the narrow streets of one of the many favelas scattered through Rio de Janeiro as it headed towards its destination. Their path took them along the base of a steep-sided mountain, which instead of being coated with verdant green was covered in concrete and tin. Anja looked up at the ghastly sight and wondered how people could exist in such a place. The man seated in front of her in the passenger seat of the vehicle, turned and said, "What is it you are looking for in Brazil, Anja?"

"A girl, Elias. An American."

"What sets her apart from the others that Medusa has taken?" Elias asked curiously.

"We were put together to find her."

"You shouldn't have come," he replied adamantly.

Anja tugged at her body armor before resting her hand back on her MP5. Everyone in the convoy, including her people were dressed as though ready for combat.

"I had to," she said.

"Rio isn't like it used to be, Anja. The favelas have

grown just like the gangs who run them. The program which brought the police to try and clean them up has failed miserably. So far this year alone, there have been one-hundred and twenty police killings."

"Then why are we here, Elias?"

"Because this is where I have my team based and where Medusa operates."

"In the favelas?"

"Yes. No one misses the girls they take off the streets. Hell, some parents even sell them their own children for as little as fifty American dollars."

Anja stared out the window as the buildings shot past. How could people even do that to their own children? "Do you know where they are based, Elias?"

"Medusa?"

"Yes."

"An old hotel which they use to hold auctions. People come from all over South America and from other countries to purchase. Some of them buy girls just to restock their brothels with fresh ones."

"What happens to the ones they don't need anymore?"

His answer was cold, brutal. "They kill them."

"How come you haven't shut it down?" Anja asked.

"We have tried, but every time we move we are shut down by some government official claiming that we have no jurisdiction there."

"So what do you actually do?" There was a coldness to her voice.

"The best we can, Anja. We do the best we can."

"If they've shipped some girls to Rio there must be an auction coming soon," the Talon commander theorized.

"I will ask around. See what my informants have to say."

"I suppose you don't know who pulls the strings at the tip of Medusa?"

"That is the million-dollar question, isn't it? I only know of the one at the head of the Rio operation. We have picked up some soldiers who are lower on the ladder, but before we can ask them too many questions they are assassinated. Somehow they know where we take them."

"It's the tattoos," Anja explained. "They have some kind of isotope in them that is able to be tracked."

"That would explain it."

The convoy bounced across an intersection then came to a hard stop. Ahead of them was a roadblock consisting of two trucks and multiple armed men. "What's going on?" Anja asked.

"Someone else knew you were coming," Elias said. "Give me a moment."

Elias climbed from the vehicle and walked forward towards the trucks. He spent a couple of minutes talking to a gray-haired officer in a pristine uniform. Arms were waved and fingers pointed before the special taskforce commander walked back towards the armored vehicle.

He climbed in the front muttering a multitude of curses. Then he turned to Anja. "You have been given twenty-four hours to leave the country. Until then you are to remain under close surveillance in our compound."

"How are we meant to find the girl and get her out if we aren't allowed to do anything?"

"You aren't."

"Who was that man?"

"Juan Bernardo. Head of the Brazilian Secret Police."

"Is he corrupt?"

Elias' answer was abrupt. "Do you think he would be here if he wasn't?"

"I'm sorry, Elias, it was a stupid question."

"No, I'm sorry. I get so frustrated with it all. I guess you have come all this way for nothing."

Anja's cell buzzed. She looked at the screen and frowned, then hit answer. "Yes."

"We have a problem," said Ilse.

"What?"

"Jake has gone."

———

WHEN THE CONVOY HAD STOPPED, Hawk could tell something was wrong. "Something's not right."

"Why do you say that?" Ilse asked.

"A feeling."

"I guess we'll find out."

"Not waiting to find out," he replied taking his body armor off.

"What are you doing?"

"Going for a walk." He checked his SIG and took spare magazines for it and put them in his pockets.

"Stay here, Jake," Ilse ordered.

"I'll be fine. I'll send you a postcard."

Before she could respond, he slipped out of the vehicle and into the alley opposite. He followed the alley —if that's what it was; more a narrow pathway between the structures. From there it turned into a maze of twists and turns. He wasn't certain of where he was headed, but if he were to ask some questions he'd likely get some answers. Besides, in communities like this, people knew everything about everything.

"Hey, what the fuck are you doing?" a thickset man wearing a stained singlet asked.

"I'm looking for a friend," Hawk lied.

"He's not around here, go away before you never leave."

"What do you know about Medusa?" Hawk asked him. "You ever heard of them?"

The man's expression changed. "Get out of here, asshole, before I kill you myself."

The man may have not answered the question

verbally, but his reaction told Hawk all he needed to know. He held up his hands placatingly. "All right, I'm going."

Hawk kept on through the maze. He'd just turned another of the blind corners when his cell buzzed. He didn't need to look at it to know who it would be. "What do you think you're doing?"

"I'm not sure yet," he replied. "When I know, I'll tell you."

"Damn it, Jacob," Anja growled. "You need to get back here. We've been given twenty-four hours to get out of the country."

Hawk stopped. "What about the girl?"

"She's out of reach."

He thought of Brussels. "The hell she is. We've come this far; I'm not leaving her behind."

"This isn't Brussels, Jake."

"You're right about that. This time I get the girl out alive."

There was a long silence as Anja contemplated her next words. "All right, Jake. Stay out of trouble. I'm going to send you some coordinates. You need to be there before dark."

"What happens then?"

"The auction starts."

"I'll be there."

"We can't help you, Jake. You're on your own."

"I work better alone," he replied and disconnected the call.

———

"I TOLD YOU TO LEAVE, PUTA," the man said from behind Hawk.

The Brit turned and saw that the man wasn't alone. He had two friends; they were all as scruffy looking as each other. All three were armed. Two had knives while the other had a baseball bat with nails sticking from it. "Come on, mates, you don't want to do this. I'm leaving. Just trying to figure out which way to go. It's a frigging rabbit warren in here."

"Too late, my friend. Give us your wallet and all of your valuables."

"And if I do that, you'll let me go, right?"

The man shrugged.

Hawk sighed. "Yeah, I thought so."

He looked at the one with the bat to the left of the leader. His first thought was that the stains on the bat was rust from the nails then realization dawned that it was a little more sinister; dried blood. "That's a nasty looking weapon you have there, cock."

The man grinned wickedly, exposing crooked yellow teeth.

Hawk's hand disappeared behind him and came out with the SIG. He centered it on the man's face, and the grin disappeared instantly. "I don't want to kill any of you, but when it comes down to me and you, I'm picking *my* side."

The three men each took a step back, obviously used to having the odds stacked in their favor. Hawk took a step forward. "Make your choice. All I want to do is leave."

They took another step back.

Hawk nodded. "All right, I'm glad we reached an understanding."

The Brit slipped back into the maze of structures and seemed to be making his way back to where he needed to be when his cell buzzed. He checked it and saw that it was the coordinates for the auction. According to the screen he still had a way to go.

Sudden movement behind him caused Hawk to pivot. He threw himself back just as a knife cut through the air where he'd just been standing. His back crashed against the wall of a shanty keeping him mostly upright.

The man with the knife stepped in, closing the distance between them. Hawk recognized him as one of the three who'd cornered him.

The man's knife hand streaked forward in a move intent on spilling Hawk's guts over the ground. The Brit twisted to the side and the knife flashed across in front of him. Hawk slashed at the man's throat with the side of his palm in a chopping motion.

The strike dealt Knifeman a devastating blow, stunning him to immobility. Hawk twisted him and clamped his hands in position on either side of Knifeman's head before twisting savagely, causing the neck to break.

He let the body fall and looked up just in time to meet the attack of the man with the wicked baseball bat.

Once more Hawk was forced back. He dropped under the second blow and swept his attacker's legs from beneath him with a solid kick.

The man howled as he fell heavily beside his dead friend. Hawk moved in close and drove the heel of his boot down into the center of the attacker's chest.

Bones splintered and the man cried out once more. The Brit bent swiftly, picked up the bat and swung it as though chopping wood. The nails embedded deeply into the man's head, killing him immediately.

Hawk yanked the bat free and turned to meet the final attacker who stopped cold when he realized that his knife couldn't stack up against the bat. "You got your friends killed, pal, you want to join them?"

The man's eyes filled with fear, and he dropped the knife and ran off.

"Didn't think so."

Hawk dropped the bat next to its dead owner and turned away, leaving them there for someone else to clean up.

MAYA WAS FEELING LIGHT-HEADED. It had been caused by the last needle they'd given her. Just enough juice to keep her mellow, not as high as a kite, for the auction. She'd been cleaned up and given a new dress to wear. It was a light blue form-hugging evening dress which accentuated all her curves.

They had told her tonight she would be sold and that there had been quite a substantial expression of interest for her from the involved parties. Bidders had come from Dubai, Saudi Arabia, Hong Kong, Slovenia, and Uzbekistan. With so much interest, they informed her that she would fetch a premium price.

Maya looked up as the door to her cell opened. She noticed the couple who entered were well-dressed in a suit and evening gown, respectively. As the woman came closer, she said, "It is time."

# CHAPTER TWELVE

*Rio de Janeiro, Brazil*

THE OUTSIDE of the hotel looked like something one would find in an abandoned city. Overgrown landscape, paint peeling from every exterior surface, fences in disrepair, and in some areas, Hawk could see lights shining through broken windowpanes. However, the small procession of vehicles into the parking lot coupled with the profusion of lights told him that at least some part of it was still functioning.

Hawk waited in the shadows, watching as the vehicles arrived. Every person stepping out of the vehicles were dressed as though they were arriving for some kind of ball or formal function. Even the armed guards were wearing tuxedos.

"I need to get myself one of those," Hawk said to himself.

He eyed the parking lot carefully, noticing with interest one of the guards in the far corner, standing his post a good distance away from the others. Keeping low and using the vehicles for cover he closed the distance between himself and the guard. Then, when the man wasn't looking, he took him from behind, breaking his neck like it was matchwood.

A few minutes later, Hawk was freshly attired in a suit, although a little big on him, he figured it would pass.

Hawk used the shadows once more to get close to the hotel. There was no way he would get past the guards on the door, so he needed to find another way in. And antici-pating that all doorways would be guarded, that left only one way. Up.

After a few minutes, Hawk found a place where he could climb up onto a first-floor balcony which ran along the front of the hotel. Once there he just walked in through the unlocked glass door. How easy could this be?

"Hold it there."

Apparently not that easy.

———

HAWK TURNED SLOWLY to stare into the beam of a bright flashlight. He put his left hand up in front of his eyes to stop the light from blinding him.

"What are you doing?" the man hissed.

"Would you believe I forgot my room key?"

"You will come with me."

The Brit shrugged. "All right, if you insist."

"Walk to the door."

The room was empty apart from what looked like a counter attached to the wall. It smelled of mildew and dust. The man stepped back, making room to allow the Brit to pass.

Hawk reached the door and walked out into the hallway which was lit by a light string from one end to the other. He stopped. "What the fuck, man, why have lights up here if you got no guests?"

Then he heard it. Groans of pleasure coming from

behind one of the doors further along the hallway. He looked at the man. "Really?"

"Get moving."

Hawk turned away and then whirled back. He knocked the gun aside with eye-watering speed and hit the man in the throat to stop him from crying out. While the man was stunned, Hawk finished him off by breaking his neck.

A moment later, the Brit was dragging the corpse back into the privacy of the room where it would be out of sight. "Wait there. Don't make a sound."

Hearing voices coming from the hallway, he waited a moment before stepping back out of sight. Male and female voices. He waited.

There was one man talking to two females, and all were speaking excitedly about the auction. The women were trying to convince the man that he had time to be with them before the auction started. "We have an hour."

"That is not enough time," the man replied. His accent sounded European.

"I guess there will be plenty of time after it is finished," the second woman said, pouting.

"All right," the man acquiesced.

From the darkness Hawk watched them walk by, his hand gripping the SIG. Then they disappeared into a room.

He tucked his SIG away and slipped out into the hallway and made his way downstairs.

———

"I HATE BEING able to do nothing," Anja growled as she crossed the room for the hundredth time.

"I'm sure Jake won't do anything stupid," Ilse replied.

Anja stopped and stared at her intel officer. Ilse nodded. "You're right, who am I trying to kid."

"What is the problem?" asked Elias.

Anja sighed. "Jake is what you would call a loose cannon. From what I can gather, a great operator, but can be reckless."

Elias frowned, concern on his face. "I see. So he is likely to—"

"—go in there alone and cause an immense amount of chaos," she finished for him.

"And get himself killed."

"There's always that."

"I'd better get my team ready."

"Wait, Elias," Anja said, placing her hand on his arm. "You can't. What about your friend?"

"Let me worry about him. I'll take my team, but you must remain here. Understood?"

She nodded. "Don't underestimate, Jake, he's quite resourceful."

"He'll need to be."

———

ONCE DOWNSTAIRS, Hawk started to mingle. The bottom floor of the hotel had been transformed into a giant ballroom with a bar and large stage. All the attendees wore identical theatrical masks to create a certain level of anonymity. It took Hawk only moments to acquire one for himself, making him look and feel like a weird freak.

As he eased his way through the crowd, a spotlight came on over the stage and all eyes turned to face it as a man stepped into its beam. He wore a personal mike beside his mouth, the wire snaking back to the piece in his ear then further on below his suit collar. He spoke charismatically, like a television evangelist, "Ladies and gentlemen, the auction will start in twenty minutes. Thank you."

A murmur rippled through the crowd, and they began

to gradual migration towards the stage. Hawk noticed that some of the women wore identical form-fitting evening gowns. Then he realized why. They were the entertainment. The hostesses who looked after the special customers. Five of them. They would be the biggest spenders, the high rollers at the casino if you like.

One of the men was dressed in a black suit, another in a Thobe which at a guess, Hawk put him as Saudi. After all, they were loaded, right? The third was resplendent in a dove-gray Gucci suit with bow tie and gold watch chain. The fourth wore a royal-blue Armani suit with a red carnation in the lapel. The fifth one had on a white Kandura. The clothing worn by UAE men. Their apparel bespoke wealth.

Using his cell, Hawk did his best to get pictures of all five then sent them all through to Ilse. He'd just sent the last when he felt a hand on his shoulder. He turned to see a woman wearing the same mask and wearing an evening gown which was split down the middle to her navel, exposing the bulge of her rounded breasts and the flawlessness of the olive skinned flat abdomen. "¿Que estas haciendo?"

Hawk stared at her before saying, "What?"

"I asked what you were doing?" she replied in lightly accented English.

Hawk shrugged. "First time. Taking in the sights."

"You know you're not allowed to have them in here?"

The Brit lifted his mask to show her his shocked expression. "Really? Crap."

The faceless woman reached out and gently put his mask back in place. "Keep it down. You really are new, aren't you?"

"Something like that."

"Are you here with anyone?"

"No, I'm on my own. The person I was meant to be here with, my boss, had to pull out at the last moment so he sent me. Apparently, he wants me to buy him an American girl. Can you believe it? Come here and buy women?"

The woman nodded.

"Couldn't show me around, could you?" Hawk asked. "Before things get underway?"

"Maybe I could," the woman replied. "What should I call you?"

Hawk opened his mouth to speak but she must have sensed it and cut him off. "For heaven's sake, don't use your real name."

He smiled at her. "I was going to say, Ronnie, as in Ronnie Barker. Ever heard of him?"

The woman shook her head. "No. You can call me, Aphrodite."

Hawk smiled at her from behind his mask. Again, she must have sensed it because she said, "No smart comments, Ronnie."

"I wouldn't dream of it," he replied. "Where will we start?"

"How about we get a glass of champagne and take it from there."

"Sounds fine. I must say, that's a nice dress you're wearing."

Aphrodite leaned in close and whispered. "No, you can't take it off me."

When she stepped back Hawk stared at her, baffled by her comment, and could see her eyes glisten with merriment through the slits in the mask. "I wouldn't have dreamed of saying such a thing," Hawk said to her.

Once more Aphrodite leaned close and said, "For what you have in mind, my dear, you won't even have to take the dress off me."

*Holy shit!*

Aphrodite guided him through the crowd toward the bar where she selected two delicate flutes of champagne for them. A fine golden straw in each glass glinted in the light, allowing the drink to be enjoyed without displacing their masks. Hawk took a sip and felt the bubbles flutter across his tongue.

The Brit leaned close to his escort and pointed at the guy in the blue suit. "Why is he dressed differently from the others?"

"What do you mean?"

"Almost everyone here is dressed the same. Like me with a black suit. The guy in the gray suit and him in the blue."

"Oh, I see what you mean," Aphrodite said. "They're some of the VIP guests."

"VIP?"

"A lot of money."

"Oh, looks like I'm wasting my time bidding tonight then," Hawk said in a melancholy voice. "My boss is going to be pissed."

"I'm sure you'll be able to find one to suit."

"Any chance of getting a look before they go on sale?"

"You've got to be kidding."

"Yeah, you're right, it was kind of hopeful. How much longer do we have?"

Aphrodite looked down at the watch on her wrist. It looked expensive with its diamond encrusted band. "Ten more minutes."

He stared at her. "What are we going to do for ten more minutes?"

She took his glass and placed it with her on the tray of a passing waiter. "Ten minutes is a long time," Aphrodite said.

"Yes, it is."

She took his hand once more and led him through the crowd to a doorway. Aphrodite tried the handle and it opened. She led Hawk into the room, closing the door behind them, turning the latch so it locked.

They were in a large lounge with leather chairs and low coffee tables.

"Wow," said Hawk, "this looks way cool."

"You can look later," Aphrodite said to him and pulled him close.

Their masks came off and their lips smashed together. Their bodies flattened against each other. Hawk broke the tongue tangle and stepped back. "Let me get rid of my coat."

As he removed it, he hid the SIG in amongst the folds. When he turned to face Aphrodite, his face crumpled into a puzzled expression. It might have had something to do with the look of displeasure on her pretty face. But mostly because of the Taurus PT92 handgun in her unwavering fist. Her top lip curled up and she said harshly, "Who are you?"

"Whoa, lady, what the fuck?" Hawk asked, feigning shock.

"Stop with the games. You do not belong here."

Suddenly it became clearer in his mind. She worked for Medusa. *Idiot.*

"Well, who are you? You have maybe one minute before I shoot you."

Hawk cocked his head to the side and took a step forward. "Why would you do that? I've done nothing wrong."

"Then tell me who you are?"

"Ronnie—"

"Your real name, imbecile," she snapped.

"Jacob Hawk."

"Why are you here?"

"Buying an American girl for my boss."

"You lie."

"How about you put the gun down and we can talk about it."

"How about I kill you!" she snarled.

Hawk flung the coat at her before she could fire. Aphrodite cried out in alarm as the item of clothing wrapped around her gun hand. Hawk moved swiftly, tearing the coat free and chopping down on the wrist. The handgun fell free, and he kicked it across the floor.

Aphrodite backed away and gathered herself, taking up a fighting stance. Hawk held up his hands and said, "Just calm down."

But there was no calming of the woman. Instead, she closed the gap between them and attacked, striking like a cornered viper. With a flurry of movement, the Brit suddenly tasted blood in his mouth. He stepped back and bunched both his hands into fists. "All right, don't say you weren't warned."

Aphrodite came at him again, launching multiple blows with hands and feet which Hawk was forced to counter with all the skills taught to him by SAS training. "Wow, you're something."

She came again, this time one blow, a kick with her right leg, got through Hawk's defenses and he found himself ass down on one of the leather chairs. However, before he could react, Aphrodite flung herself at him and landed on his lap.

Her forehead came forward and connected with the bridge of his nose. Blinding lights flashed before Hawk's eyes. His vision was blurred instantly, and blood began to leak from the injured nose.

"Fuck me, what did you do that for?" he blurted out as he grabbed her slim waist and thrust her away.

Aphrodite flew backward, her light frame no burden for Hawk to throw. She crashed down on a glass-topped coffee table, shattering it. Groaning, she rolled away, climbing to her feet, blood running from an open wound in her side.

A knife appeared in her right hand. Hawk frowned. "Now, where the bloody hell did you get that?"

"It's what I'm going to do with it that counts," she hissed.

Aphrodite came in flicking the knife back and forth. Hawk leaped back just as a scything blow came in with lightning speed. He gasped as he felt the bite of the blade. Nothing too bad, but he needed to end this before the woman cut him to ribbons, and he didn't need that.

"I warned you, didn't I?" he growled. "Silly fucking cow. Now you've given me no choice."

Hawk circled around to his right, Aphrodite following his every move. Not taking his eyes from her, he leaned down and picked up the solid wooden leg of the broken coffee table. Just as he did, the woman moved, closing the gap between them with surprising speed.

But the Brit was just that little bit quicker and as he came up, he lashed out with the leg and caught the wild-eyed woman a blow to her knife arm.

Instant numbness caused her to drop the weapon as she cried out in pain. Hawk stepped in closer and swung the leg again, this time catching her up the side of the head. She dropped where she'd stood, and sucking in deep breaths, Hawk leaned down beside her to check her pulse. He gave a grunt of satisfaction. "You'll wake up with a headache, but at least you'll wake up. That's more than you would have done for me with that knife." Wood tended to be more forgiving than a harder material like steel.

Hawk checked his wound and wiped the blood from his face on a napkin he found on the table. He picked up the knife and checked Aphrodite for the sheath. Once he recovered it, he housed the weapon and put it in the back of his pants. Then he straightened his clothing and prepared to walk out into the hall. The auction was about to start.

———

"GOOD EVENING, LADIES AND GENTLEMEN!" the voice boomed from the stage in accented English. "Welcome to another gala evening where we the people of Medusa hope to fulfil your every need."

"So much for being covert," Hawk muttered.

One thing could be said about Medusa; they had many things in their arsenal to keep people silent, but the one most utilized was fear. Should that not work, however, then any and all threats were neutralized without prejudice. This business model had seen them explode to a worldwide conglomeration of multifarious activities under the control of one man.

The speaker continued. "Now, without further ado, I would like to present the first of our items for this evening."

There was movement off stage and a woman and man appeared escorting forward a girl in a black formal dress. Her dark hair was coiffed immaculately, and her makeup had been applied by a professional. To Hawk she seemed somehow too compliant for someone about to be sold into sexual slavery. Realization hit him. She was drugged. The expression on the face, the lost look in her eyes. "Fucking wankers," he growled softly as he took out his cell to capture a picture.

The man—who obviously doubled as the auctioneer—stepped up beside her. "Here we have a lovely young lady from Canada. Who will start the bidding at one-hundred thousand dollars?"

No one moved.

"Come, come, ladies and gentlemen, she is worth every bit of the opening price and more."

Still nothing.

The auctioneer stepped behind the dazed girl, doing something to her dress. Hawk frowned, wondering what he was up to. He had his answer within moments as the dress fell in a soft pool around her ankles, exposing firm breasts and black underwear.

The man stepped back out into the open and said, "How about now?"

With a flurry, no less than five hands shot into the air and the bidding began in earnest. By the time they were done, the girl from Canada had been sold for $250,000.

Hawk suddenly found himself trying to formulate a plan to rescue her and anyone else that needed it. But it was a foolhardy exercise; there was no way he would get them all out on his own.

The next one was brought into the spotlight from the backstage area where the Canadian girl had just been taken. Hawk immediately felt his stomach churn. This girl had skin the color of burnished copper. "Shit."

"Now ladies and gentlemen, we have a beauty from Jamaica. Such a delectable morsel—well you get my meaning. But such beauty commands a higher price. Shall we start at five-hundred thousand?"

Immediately the buyer from the UAE put his hand up. It was followed by a flurry of bidding and the price soon rose to $850,000. That was when another bidder raised their hand and shouted, "One million dollars!"

A hush enveloped the crowd as all eyes locked on a woman in the center of the room. Like everyone around her, her mask hid her face. But it couldn't disguise the long, flowing, blonde hair that danced down her naked back where the cut of her red dress revealed a cleft of tanned skin at the top of her firm buttocks.

"Well, well, well!" the auctioneer exclaimed. "That is a bid."

"Do you accept it?" the woman asked, her accent undeniably French.

"Let me see." The auctioneer looked around the crowd but saw no further bids to persuade him otherwise. "Madam's bid is accepted. Congratulations."

The Jamaican girl was taken from the stage and Hawk saw the French woman begin making her way to a door on the west side of the ballroom. Edging his way through the crowd, he began to follow her.

"Now, for the next item," the auctioneer called out.

Hawk stopped to look. It was another white girl. Not Maya. Torn about what to do, he headed after the woman in the red dress who was now disappearing through the door.

The door led to a long hallway. By the time Hawk reached it, the woman was turning a corner at the far end.

The Brit catfooted along the hallway trying to make no noise. A trait left over from his days as an operator. When he reached the end, he made the turn. This time the hallway was shorter; and empty.

At the end of the corridor stood an open doorway with stairs leading down. When Hawk reached the landing, he stopped and listened. The sound of a door closing told him all he needed to know, and he began a cautious descent.

The stairwell circled around until it reached what appeared to be a fire door. Hawk pushed it open to find a large, dimly lit basement type room on the other side. He couldn't see anyone but could hear voices. He crept across to a stack of boxes where he sheltered, listening.

Hawk heard the catch on the door behind him snick open and saw an armed man come through the opening.

Hawk crouched as low as he could and moved furtively into the shadows out of sight. The man walked around the boxes and into the main basement area. The voices continued uninterrupted until the sound of a protesting female voice reached Hawk's ears.

"Don't touch me!"

"You will do as I say!" The French woman. "Give her some more drugs."

They must have another way down here, the Brit thought. Another stairwell or maybe an elevator.

"We can't give her any more just yet."

"What about something to knock her out?"

"Later, before you leave."

"Alright then."

"Put her back in her cell," the man ordered. "They're waiting upstairs for the next one. I think it's the American this time. The blonde one."

Hawk reached into his mind for the picture he knew was there. It came to him, and he nodded. Maya Jones had blonde hair. He positioned himself so he could see the speakers. The French woman he knew. The guard who came through after him, then there were three other men and another woman.

The French woman stood near a man at a laptop. He was busy tapping keys before turning it to face the woman in the red dress. She leaned down and tapped the keys. *Money transfer.*

She straightened up and Hawk heard her say, "Alright?"

"Looks good."

A guard appeared escorting the blonde American. As he thought, it was the girl they were here for. Maya Jones.

"My, my, aren't you special?" the French woman cooed. Hawk saw her reach out a hand and trail it across Maya's arm before letting her fingers trace across the exposed chest skin. "I think I might have to buy you too. Then I will have my ebony and ivory."

"This one will go for more than just a million," the man behind the computer said.

"I can afford it."

A phone on the desk near the computer buzzed. The man picked it up. "Yes."

He listened and then hung up. "They're ready for her."

It was time to act.

Hawk looked around his feet for anything he could

utilize. There was a short iron bar on the floor and he picked it up. Turning quickly, he moved to the door behind him and dropped the bar into the brackets there for just that purpose. Then he drew the SIG and stepped out into the open.

# CHAPTER THIRTEEN

*Rio de Janeiro, Brazil*

UNFORTUNATELY, with no way of doing it quietly, he hoped that given the distance they were from anyone else, no one would hear what was about to happen. As soon as Hawk exposed himself, the nearest man looked up, startled. He moved for his weapon just as the Brit shot him.

The sound of the gun going off made Hawk's ears ring. Immediately dropping to the hard floor, a spray of blood erupted from the man's wound. Hawk changed his aim and shot the next man in line as he scrambled for his weapon. The guard fell back, and Hawk snarled, "Hold it!"

Both women froze on the spot with the sudden onset of violence. The three remaining men stared at Hawk and then gave panicked glances to each other. Knowing what they were thinking, the Brit growled, "Don't do it," giving them fair warning.

The man behind the laptop reached for something and Hawk shot him. One bullet; in the head. "Damn it."

The remaining men raised their hands.

Hawk hurried forward and relieved them of their

weapons. He glanced at Maya who seemed to be unmoved. "Are you alright?"

"Huh?"

"Alright! Are you alright?"

"Huh?"

"Fuck me." He turned to one of the men. "What did you give her?"

"I—I don't know." He glanced at the fair-haired woman.

Hawk pointed his gun at her. "Talk."

"It's just something to take the edge off. Makes them more compliant. It'll wear off in thirty minutes."

"Alright, let's get you lot locked away. Where do you keep the girls?"

"Back there."

"Get moving."

Leaving Maya where she was, he followed them, ushering them into a vacant cell, but before he did he stopped the French woman. "You, wait there."

She stopped and turned to face him. Hawk took her mask off revealing a pretty face with flawless skin. He held up his cell and said, "Smile."

He took the picture, kept the mask, and said, "Now you can go."

"I will not forget you," she hissed.

He gave her a crooked grin. "Nor I you."

Hawk locked them away and hurried back to where Maya stood waiting. He looked her over, her gaze still vacant. He tapped her gently on the face. "Hey, you with me?"

"What?"

"I said are you with me?"

"Who are you?"

"A friend."

"Huh?"

He held out the mask. "Put this on."

"Why?"

"Just do it."

"Who are you?"

Hawk shook his head. "Jesus Christ. Put the bloody mask on."

Once it was fitted, he said, "Now, do what I say."

"Why?"

"Listen, do you want to die. Because—I give up. Don't move."

Hawk hurried over to the desk and picked up the laptop. He found the bag it had been housed in and zipped it up. He slung the strap over his shoulder and bent to retrieve one of the guards' weapons, an MP7. He also gathered a spare magazine to go with it. Then Hawk walked back to Maya. "Hey, look at me."

She turned her head, and he lifted the mask for another quick look. "Do everything I say."

Maya nodded. That was a good sign.

Once the mask was lowered back into place, he grabbed her arm and guided her to the elevator. The doors slid open, and they entered. Instead of hitting the button for ground floor, he pressed the one that would take them to the first level.

The elevator rose smoothly and as it reached the ground level where the auction was, Hawk held his breath momentarily hoping it wouldn't stop. When it didn't, he let out a long breath.

The elevator slowed and Hawk eased Maya to the side. "What are you doing?"

"Just stay against the wall," he told her as he raised the MP7 to his shoulder.

The doors slid open to reveal an empty hallway. Hawk stepped out and swept both directions before holding out his hand for his charge. "Remember, stay behind me. Put your hand in the middle of my back and don't move it."

"Who are you?" Maya asked for the tenth time; the tone of her voice, however, was more alert.

"Listen, my name is Jake. I'm here to get you out. Do you understand?"

She nodded.

"Good, now do as I tell you."

He turned away from her and felt her place her hand in the middle of his back. "How are we going to get out of here?"

He started to answer when one of the doors further along the hallway opened. He whirled and rushed Maya towards the nearest open doorway opposite their position. "Move," he whispered harshly.

Once inside, Hawk stood near the doorway and listened. He heard the lighthearted laugh of a woman followed by a man's voice who seemed to be protesting something. Hawk then realized who they were, especially when the second female voice joined the others. It was the threesome he'd encountered earlier. So much for making the auction.

He waited for the voices to recede and then stepped out into the hall once more. He was all too aware that once the traffickers realized that Maya was missing, all they had to do was track her.

He stuck his head back into the room. "All right, come on."

With Maya behind him, Hawk commenced the arduous feat of getting out of there alive. They made it along the hallway and were going into the room by which he'd gained access. They could go out over the balcony. That was the plan.

It all changed when the elevator opened behind them, and two armed men stepped out.

———

"THERE!"

Hawk spun around, immediately spotting the pair of armed men, the closest one pointing in their direction. "Get down!" he barked at Maya.

He brought up the MP7 and fired just as the lead shooter did the same. Bullets cracked. Hawk winced as he felt one burn past his face. Hawk's burst stitched a line of bullets diagonally across the shooter's chest leaving it bloody. The falling man crashed into his friend knocking his weapon askew, giving the Brit the time he needed to deal with him.

Another burst of fire and the second shooter cried out and buckled at the knees.

Hawk grabbed Maya who was crying, terrified at the violence she'd just witnessed. "Get up," he snapped. "Hurry! That gunfire will bring more."

The Talon agent pulled his charge into the room they would escape through. The sound of shouts reached his ears as he guided Maya out of the way so he could close the door behind them. Crossing the room he stepped out onto the long balcony.

Looking below, he checked to make sure it was clear before hurrying back to Maya. He tilted her chin up so she was looking at him, then said, "Come on, we have to climb down."

"In this—" she ripped the mask free. "In this thing?"

Hawk removed his own mask and nodded. The dress she was wearing would make it almost impossible. "You're right."

He grabbed the knife he'd taken from Aphrodite and hacked at the fabric midthigh. "There, now climb—"

He heard the door crash back in the room they'd just vacated. "Climb down, hurry."

Without so much as a question, Maya started to climb over the rail.

Hawk rushed to the glass sliding door of the room and

sprayed the inside with gunfire from the MP7. The weapon ceased to fire mid sweep and he was forced to throw himself to one side as a hailstorm of bullets erupted from the gunmen within. He scrambled to the wall, placing his back against the rough surface. He changed out the spent magazine for the fresh one, worked the cocking lever, and went back to work.

Hawk leaned around the corner and fired at a shooter who was trying to bull his way through, his weapon up ready to shoot. Hawk brought him down with a short burst that stopped him in his tracks.

The action infuriated those within the room's confines and a fresh barrage of fire issued forth.

Hawk ducked back before glancing in the direction he'd last seen Maya. She'd disappeared over the balcony. The Brit leaned around to check before blowing off the rest of the magazine. Once it was dry, he tossed the weapon aside and ran for the rail.

———

AS HE SAILED over the railing, Hawk reached out with his right hand, grasping for a hold. His fingers caught and the momentum swung him down until he crashed into the side of the balcony. Pain shot through his chest and side causing him to cry out. If his rib wasn't broken before, it definitely was now. His instant reaction was to let go so that he fell the rest of the way to the ground below.

"Are you all right?" Maya asked him in an urgent whisper.

Hawk groaned. "Never felt better."

He grabbed the strap for the laptop bag. "Here, take this."

"Shouldn't we get going?"

Sucking in deep breaths he managed to say, "You go, let me die here."

Maya grabbed his shirt. "Get up. Move."

Hawk groaned and got up with her help. He'd only just reached his feet when the shooters appeared above them. "There they are!"

Guns opened fire and the ground around them was peppered with bullets. "Fuck!" Hawk snarled. He grabbed Maya and started to drag her towards the overgrown garden in front of them.

The unkempt shrubs and trees closed around them like a jungle, enveloping them in its foliage. Rounds followed them in and started pruning branches like a crazed hedge trimmer. "Get down," Hawk growled, pushing Maya down onto her front. He followed her and lay there as angry hornets decimated the garden's undergrowth. The girl held her hands over her head and Hawk could feel her flinch every time a round came close.

"We have to get out of here," he said into her ear as he reached for his SIG.

"How?"

"Just keep your head down and run."

"But—"

"It's our only chance. Ready?"

"No."

"Now—go!"

They both burst free of the overgrown garden, running away from the rundown hotel. A shout from above and the shooters shifted their aim. They took cover behind what had once been a large, concrete, raised garden bed.

Bullets smacked into it as the pair crouched low, taking deep breaths. Hawk looked ahead of them at the parking lot. "We have to make it to the car park," he shouted at her over the noise. "Ready?"

"I—I can't."

"Yeah you, can, love. Just put your head down and run like hell. Go!"

Once more Maya was running for her life. By now the effect of the drugs in her system had worn off, replaced by an almost uncontrollable fear. She screamed at the top of her voice as she ran across the drive and continued towards the lot.

Behind her, Hawk was a lot calmer. He kept his head on a swivel as he traced her footsteps. Had he not done so, the two shooters who appeared to their right would have been overlooked.

Hawk stopped abruptly and brought his SIG around, firing three times and watching the first of the pair stop as though hit by a large hammer. Falling to the ground, the body almost tripped up his friend who was directly behind him.

The Brit started to walk to his left, moving in the direction of the lot. He fired four more rounds at the second shooter, relieved when he saw the man's leg buckle beneath him. Crying out, the man clutched at the wound in his upper thigh.

Looking about once more, Hawk began to sprint towards the car park. In front of him, Maya cried out as she tripped and fell.

His heart rate spiked, and he called out, "Maya!"

Coming to her side, he crouched as more bullets cracked overhead. "Are you alright?"

"My ankle. I twisted it."

"Shit." He scooped her up and threw her over his shoulder as he would a sack of wheat.

"What are you doing?" Maya cried out.

"You can't bloody stay here," Hawk replied as he started to jog. "You know, you could stand to lose a few pounds."

"Thanks a lot."

One of the armed parking lot attendants appeared behind a vehicle at Hawk's ten o'clock. A burst of fire emanated from his automatic weapon, making Hawk pause and grab Maya, dragging her down behind an SUV. Bullets punched into the vehicle's thin skin, the rounds demolishing door linings and upholstery. The side windows blew out sending glass spraying across the pair. Hawk fired more rounds until his weapon ran dry, dropping out the empty magazine and replacing it with his reserve.

Waiting until the shooter had stopped firing, Hawk rose instantly and put a bullet in the man's chest. Grabbing Maya's hands from her ears, he spoke softly, "Keep down and follow me."

Although it was dark there was still an ambient light from the hotel. They started weaving their way through the mass of parked vehicles. As he went, the Brit checked a door on each car, hoping. But they were all locked.

Shouts echoed throughout the parking lot as the hunters guided each other towards their target. Hawk stopped Maya behind a Mercedes. "Keep down. Don't say anything."

He crouched beside her, his left hand on her arm hoping it would have a calming effect upon her. Hawk could feel her trembling. He leaned close and whispered into her ear, "Trust me."

They remained in their crouched positions, even when the shooting died away. An eerie silence enveloped the parking lot, and Hawk imagined the shooters were closing in on them, using hand signals. That's what he would have done with his men. He listened intently, his right hand tightening its grip on the SIG.

Hawk could feel his heart racing in his chest. He whispered to Maya, "Whatever happens, don't get up."

After what seemed like an eternity, the sound of a footfall on gravel triggered Hawk's reaction. He came up with a fist full of handgun and found his target no more than a couple of meters from where he was. He squeezed the trigger once. There was no reason to do it again. Not at that distance. Instantly, he began scanning the lot for his next target, knowing when he locked eyes on it he was too late.

Hawk went limp at his knees allowing his weight to take him down. Once more automatic gunfire ripped through the air. "Shit!"

Beside him Maya jerked and spasmed with every round that impacted the vehicle. Hawk covered her with his arms as the firing intensified. They were pinned down and there appeared to be no way out for either of them.

With bullets flying everywhere, Hawk sat down and wrapped an arm around her shoulders, pulling her in close.

Suddenly an explosion ripped through the parking lot and three TUPI light armored 4x4s rolled into view. Armed men alighted and formed a perimeter around the vehicles, firing their weapons and driving the shooters back.

"Jake? Where are you?" a voice called.

Hawk stood up slowly. "Over here."

The man hurried across to him. It wasn't until he was standing beside them that Hawk realized who it was. "Elias?"

"Hurry. We—who is that?"

"Maya Jones, the girl we were after. Listen, there's more girls inside."

"I'm aware of that but we must leave now."

"Hold on, mate. Didn't you hear what I said?"

Elias placed a hand on Hawk's shoulder. "I heard you, now get in the vehicle."

The Brit shook it off. "The hell I will. We have to get the other girls out."

Elias' gaze hardened. "I shouldn't even be here. Wouldn't be if it wasn't for your boss. Now get in the fucking vehicle or I will leave you both here."

There was something about Elias' gaze telling Hawk

that the man would do exactly as he said. "All right, but what about the others?"

"There's nothing we can do."

Hawk and Maya were ushered into one of the TUPIs, and they settled in while Elias made a call on his comms, his team withdrawing their positions and loading once more into the vehicles. From there they evacuated the area, leaving the rest of the prisoners to their fate.

———

"WHAT THE HELL was that load of bloody bollocks?" Hawk snarled at Anja who was talking to Ilse as he stormed into the room.

"I beg your pardon?" the Talon commander asked. "I know you're not talking to me that way, Jacob. Not if you want to stay part of this team."

Ilse glared at him as if to say pull your head in, but he ignored the silent reprimand. He put the computer bag down on the table. "We left behind women who were being trafficked there. Sold like they were frigging pieces of meat. We could have got them all out."

Anja turned her gaze to Maya Jones. "Ilse, will you please see to our guest? Jacob, come with me."

She turned away, heading for a doorway that led to another room. When they were gone, Harvey piped up from where he was sitting, "He's screwed."

Ilse sighed. "She'll certainly put him in his place. I've seen that expression before." She looked at Maya. "Come with me, I'll take care of you."

Slamming the door behind him, Hawk made it abundantly clear that he was not happy with the situation, leaving the walls trembling in his wake. Anja whirled on her operator, eyes sparking with anger. "If you ever address me in that manner in front of anyone ever again,

I'll send you scuttling back under that rock where you were found. Do you understand me, Sergeant?"

Stunned by her furious outburst, Hawk double blinked and opened his mouth to speak. Before he could, Anja snapped, "Just shut up and listen. We couldn't do anything because the security services are all over us. We are under orders from the government to get out tomorrow. Elias risked everything to get you out of there. Now, I realize that there were numerous other victims of Medusa's trade there, however, we have no choice but to focus on the long game. Be thankful that you were able to get Maya Jones out. She was our main priority. Mission success."

"I thought we were put together to take down Medusa?"

"That is the plan."

"Then what happened?"

"This is just the start."

Reaching into his pocket, Hawk took out his cell and tossed it to Anja, saying, "There are some pictures on there, but only one that will be any good. However, there are pictures of two girls they were selling. One was sold to a French woman. That's the picture I mentioned."

"I'll have Ilse take a look."

"I also brought back the computer they were using to transfer money."

Anja smiled, all hint of her anger gone. "Show me."

Retracing their footsteps into the main room, Hawk crossed to where he'd deposited the computer bag and picked it up. He looked around the room. "Where's the boy genius?"

"Harvey?"

The big operator came over to them. Anja handed him the bag and then said, "Get this to Ilse and find Jimmy. We've got a long night ahead of us."

"Yes, ma'am."

Minutes later, Jimmy was seated at a desk with the laptop in front of him. His fingers danced across the keys, his face lit up by a beatific smile. "Whoever encrypted this needs to have their ass kicked. Sloppy, very sloppy work."

Anja and Hawk stood behind him and watched him work.

"What do you have?"

"Bank accounts where money was transferred to and from. This one here," he said pointing at the screen. "Belongs to some shell company in France."

Hawk grinned. "Empty it."

"What do you want me to do with it?"

"How much is there?" Anya asked.

"A little over six-hundred million."

Hawk gave a low whistle.

"Can you set up a holding account somewhere to transfer it into?" Anja asked.

"Yes, ma'am."

"How long?"

"A few minutes," Jimmy replied.

"Do it."

A couple of minutes later he hit the enter key and said, "Done."

"What about the other accounts?" Hawk asked.

"They're all from one company but with different European banks."

"How much money altogether?" Anja asked.

"Twenty-five, thirty billion."

"Okay," said Hawk.

"Each."

"Holy shit."

"It has to be Medusa's accounts," Anja said with certainty.

"Quite possible."

"Can you get it?"

"Let me look."

Jimmy went back to work, and Anja looked at Hawk. "If we can access all Medvedev's finances it should draw him out."

"Sounds like a plan."

"I think I can do it," Jimmy said. "Do you want me to give it a go?"

"You don't sound too positive," Anja said.

"It looks straight forward to me, but often when it seems too good to be true then it's too good to be true."

Anja stared at Hawk and then back at Jimmy. "Let's wake him up."

Jimmy went back to work, his fingers punching keys on the board with practiced ease. "All right, I'm in." His finger paused above the enter key momentarily before stabbing down.

The screen went dark before coming back up. Jimmy's eyes took in every flash, every code, every line of what skipped across the screen. His lips peeled back in a smile for just a moment before it crumpled into a look of concern. "No, no, no. Shit!"

His fingers suddenly flew at breakneck speed as he tried to remedy what was happening. Behind him, Anja asked, "What is it?"

"Once the account started to empty, the others began to empty as well."

"That's good, right?" asked Hawk.

"No. I didn't do it."

"What do you mean?" Anja asked.

"It's some kind of failsafe program. If one account suddenly gets emptied or even frozen it triggers another program which withdraws the rest, transferring them to different accounts. In this case it was a certain amount."

"Where did it go?" Anja asked.

Jimmy shook his head. "I don't know. I can't even stop it happening let alone track where it's going."

"What about the account you started on?" Hawk asked.

"It's gone too. It cut off after we reached one-hundred million." He kept tapping at the keys.

"Bollocks," Hawk growled.

"That's not the worst of it."

"It gets worse?"

"Uh, huh. When this happened, it would have sent up flags across the whole system. For a moment we were visible."

Anja nodded slowly. "So they know where we are and what we've done?"

"Pretty much."

"They knew that anyway," Hawk said. "The isotope, remember?"

"Yes, but we just hacked their system and tried to steal all their money. Medvedev won't let that fly. We need to get out now."

"What about the isotope tattoo?" Hawk asked.

"It has to be neutralized."

"How?" Hawk demanded.

"Someone will have to remove it."

"You're having a laugh," Hawk said shocked at the suggestion.

His boss just stared at him, her face passive.

It was at that moment he realized she was indeed serious. "Christ, which stupid bastard's going to do it?"

Again, the stare.

"Now I know you're having a laugh. I can't do it."

"You've had triage field training; I know you have."

"That was frigging donkey's ages ago. What about the others?"

"You're here. It needs to be done now before they can zero in on us."

Hawk looked around the room and saw Elias. "Hey, Elias! Over here."

"Damn it, Jake, we're wasting time," Anja growled.

Elias joined them. "What is it?"

"Do you have a medic?"

"No."

"Fuck."

"What's going on?"

Anya gave him the ten-word version. When she was done, he said, "I'll have my men stand-to. But if you're going to do this, then you need to do it now. Medusa won't send their men; they'll have the Brazilian military do it for them."

Anja turned her gaze back to Hawk. "Well?"

"Ah, bollocks."

# CHAPTER FOURTEEN

*Dubai*

OIL SLICK FINGERS dug into Medvedev's back muscles, eliciting a low moan of pleasure. The masseuse moved her hands lower and used more pressure. This time Medvedev tensed, sending a clear message to the woman without the need to speak. Immediately she stopped. "I'm sorry, sir. Did I push too hard?"

"No, it's all right. Old injury. Please continue." He'd discovered the joy of the early morning outdoor massage last time he was in Dubai. The day was breaking to the east, the air fresh and cool. Once the sun began clawing its way across the sky, all that would change. And since he'd arrived mere hours before, the massage invigorated his travel weary muscles.

He took a deep breath as she continued, releasing the tension in his shoulders with every exhale. His cell buzzed and Medvedev muttered a curse while reaching out and scooping it up. He pressed the answer button. "Yes?"

"It is me, Viktor." Leonid.

"What is the problem?" he demanded.

"I—there—"

"Spit it out, Viktor. I already know it's something bad. Why else would you be calling at this time?"

"Someone triggered the failsafe on the bank accounts thirty minutes ago."

Medvedev sat up and looked at the dark-haired masseuse. "Go."

She wiped her hands and left.

"What happened?"

"There was an incident in Brazil—"

"What incident?" Medvedev asked, cutting his man short.

Leonid explained all he knew about what had gone wrong.

"One man took the girl and a computer which was then used to hack into my accounts? Is that correct?"

"Yes, sir. But the failsafe worked as it was designed to do."

"Yes, but it has a trigger point," the Russian pointed out. "How much did they get?"

"One-hundred million."

One-hundred million was a drop in a much larger ocean, however it was the fact that it had happened. "Was it the same people from Mexico, Leonid?"

"It is most likely."

"I want to know who they are."

"We can do better than that, we know *where* they are. The isotope on the girl they took is active. If you give the word, Viktor, I can have the necessary forces directed to the exact coordinates."

"Do it."

"Yes, sir."

"What about Rogov and his team?"

"They are on their way back to Europe."

"A waste of time seeing as the matter will be cleared up in Brazil, is it not?"

"Shall we see what plays out before we make a decision on what to do with them, Viktor?" Leonid asked.

Medvedev frowned. "Do you not have faith in our Brazilian friends, Leonid?"

"More to the point, do you, Viktor?"

"All right. We shall see what happens. Was there anything else?"

"No."

Medvedev disconnected the call. "Whoever you are, you will pay."

———

*Rio de Janeiro, Brazil*

Hawk took the scalpel and doused it with alcohol. "What are you doing?" Anja asked.

"That's how they do it in the movies," he replied.

"This isn't a damned movie, Jake."

Hawk looked down at the semi naked Maya. He could see the fear in her eyes. He held out the bottle of Cachaça. "Here, drink this."

"No—I—"

"Drink it. It'll take some of the edge off."

"Isn't there another way?"

The Brit nodded. "There is, but I don't think you would fit in a microwave. Drink."

Maya took the bottle and took a long drink. When she was done, she pulled a face. "That's terrible."

"Drink more."

Another mouthful.

"For the love of God, drink more. This is going to hurt like a bitch and the last thing I need is you moving around."

"Don't you have something that will knock me out?" she pleaded.

"You're drinking it," Hawk replied.

A trembling hand forced the bottle to her lips once more. Hawk looked at Anja and then Ilse. "You need to hold her tight and not let go."

Both gave stoic nods.

"All right." He took the bottle away from Maya and asked, "How are you feeling?"

"A little lightheaded."

"Good." He sat the bottle down beside the table where they were about to perform the operation. "Let's get started."

Before anyone realized what had happened, Hawk's bunched fist had clipped Maya on the jaw. Her eyes rolled back, and she went limp.

"What the hell, Jake?" Ilse asked, shocked.

"Do you really think that she would stay still while I cut a piece out of her hide. Let's get this done before she wakes up." He glanced at Anja who gave him a distasteful look. "Don't you start."

———

"IS EVERYTHING READY?" Anja asked Harvey.

"Yes, ma'am."

She nodded and glanced at Ilse who was helping a sore and sorry Maya to one of the vehicles. "Let's get out of here then."

They all loaded into the TUPIs. There were six in total. They would escort the Talon operators to their departure field to make sure they arrived safe and sound.

Each person in the convoy was armed and wore body armor. Wanting to be prepared for whatever might come their way. There was no way they could be prepared for what *did* come their way.

As they traveled at best speed through the favela, the lead TUPI exploded in a ball of orange flame, the only warning something was amiss was the telltale contrail from a rocket propelled grenade.

Pursuant to the first explosion, the rear TUPI was also engulfed, and suddenly the convoy went from six to four.

The intercoms of Elias' team lit up as a storm of bullets began hammering the stationary vehicles. "Dismount! Form a perimeter."

Doors were flung open, and Hawk suddenly realized what they were doing. "Hey! Stay in the vehicle. Stay in here—fuck!"

The driver's right foot had only just touched the pavement when three rounds punched into the exposed parts of his body. He grunted and slipped the rest of the way out. Meanwhile on the passenger side, the second of their escorts was also dismounting. Hawk leaned forward and tried to pull him back, to no avail, and the man suffered the same fate as his comrade.

Between him and Ilse in the back stood the third of their escort who already had the 7.62 caliber machinegun up and running.

Hawk pressed the transmit button on his comms. "Alpha One don't let them dismount! Keep them inside the vehicles! The cars are armored."

The comms crackled and there was no response. The Brit slapped his thigh. "Cock!"

He looked at Ilse. "Keep trying to get the boss. We need to get this thing moving again."

"Where are you going?" she asked him.

"Don't frigging ask," he snapped and flung open the door.

Bullets hammered the side of the TUPI as he slammed the door closed. He squatted beside the dead passenger and picked up the man's Heckler & Koch G36C. Checking the load, he grabbed a couple of magazines, stuffing them in his pockets.

A bullet cracked past Hawk's head confirming just

how precarious his position was. He spun on his heel and found a target in a narrow alley. The man was dressed in fatigues. Hawk brought up the G36 and fired. The selector was on burst and only two rounds emerged from the barrel. He cursed and flicked the selector around to auto and tried again.

This time the weapon roared defiantly, and four rounds tore into the shooter. Hawk crouched down near the fender of the vehicle in front of him as gunfire and shouts filled the humid air.

The Brit went to his comms. "Grizz, where are you?"

"Second vehicle."

"On my way."

As he ran past one of Elias' men, he tapped him on the shoulder. "Hey, get back in the fucking vehicle."

The man glanced at him and was immediately hit in the head by an incoming round. "Shit!" Hawk growled before continuing forward.

He found Harvey and Nemo Kent working together covering each other's back. Hawk knelt beside him and said loudly, "We need to get these pricks back in their vehicles before we all get killed."

"Be my guest," Harvey growled firing off the last of his magazine. "Changing!"

A shooter appeared on the rooftop of a building and was about to open fire when Hawk caught sight of him. Harvey was still reloading and exposed. Hawk's G36 came around and his finger depressed the trigger and 5.56 rounds spewed forth. The shooter disappeared from his position from the precipice.

"Get ready to roll when I give you the word," Hawk said.

"Roger that."

The Brit pushed forward until he found Anja sheltering with Elias, like Harvey and Kent, they were covering each other's backs. He was about to speak when his comms came to life. "RPG!"

There was a whoosh overhead followed by a shattering explosion. Hawk felt the heat wash over him as the fireball lifted skyward. After he recovered, he tapped Anja on the shoulder. She moved her head closer to his while still firing her weapon.

"We need to get everyone back in the vehicles before they're all killed," Hawk shouted.

"And go where?"

"Leave that up to me. But if we stay here, we're screwed."

Anja nodded abruptly. "All right."

Hawk turned to Elias. "Get your people back in the vehicles, we're getting out of here."

"I have wounded. I will not leave them."

Hawk grabbed him by the collar. "Listen, shithead. Get them frigging loaded or stay here and die."

"Jake," Anja shouted. "Go, I'll take care of it."

"Make sure you do. I'm not waiting. Where's Maya?"

"Back there. Next Tupi."

Hawk started back along the line of vehicles. When he reached Harvey he said, "Load up, we're getting the hell out of here."

"About damn time."

"Use the next one up, Grizz. Take care of the girl."

"Roger that."

"Just make sure you're on my ass when we leave."

"I'll be so far up it you'll think you've got an oversized enema tickling your spine."

When Hawk reached the TUPI where he'd left Ilse, he found her crouched over the machine gunner who was bleeding from a wound in his throat. When the door opened, she whirled and almost shot Hawk with her P226. "Shit, Jake. Have you ever heard of knocking?"

"Let's go, you're driving."

"What about this man?"

Hawk looked at him. "He's done, Ilse. He won't survive another minute."

"Jake—"

"Ilse, let him go."

"Shit," she hissed and climbed through to the driver's seat.

"You ever driven one of these things?" Hawk asked.

"Yes, I used to own one," Ilse shot back at him.

"Really?"

"No, don't be a dick."

Hawk grinned. "You ready?"

"Where are we going?" Ilse asked as bullets plinked off the armored exterior.

"Doesn't it have a GPS?"

"I don't know, Jake. Do I look like I know what I'm doing?"

"Pull forward next to the next Tupi."

Ilse got the vehicle started and stomped on the gas. It lurched forward then stopped next to the one in front of it. Hawk flung the door open and opened the one opposite. Jimmy was crouched down with his arms over his head. "Hey, kid, I need you to come with me."

He looked at Hawk in amazement. "Out there?"

"That's right. Come on."

"Are you crazy?"

"Move, damn your eyes."

Jimmy scooted across the back and into the void between the two TUPIs. Hawk opened the door and Jimmy balked. "There's a wounded guy in there."

"No, he's dead, now get the fuck in."

Hawk shoved him in through the opening and followed him inside. He called across to Ilse. "Get us out of here. Kid, we need a route to the plane."

"All right, all right."

Ilse started the TUPI moving forward. Hawk said into his comms. "This is Bravo One to all callsigns. We're moving."

"Bravo One, Alpha One. Copy. Out."

Hawk climbed into the turret where the machinegun was. He racked the bolt making sure there was a fresh round in the breach and then opened fire.

Behind the wheel, Ilse swung to the right, bumping up onto the sidewalk. She flinched every time a round struck the windscreen, depressing the gas pedal further which made the TUPI roar louder. In the turret she could hear Hawk releasing steady bursts of fire with the turret gun.

Ahead of her through the smoke stood the burning wreck of the vehicle which had been struck first. Her foot reflexively came off the pedal and the TUPI slowed. "Keep going!" Hawk shouted from above. "Stick the boot into the bitch."

Once again Ilse trod hard on the gas pedal. Even though the TUPI had only a top speed of 100KPH, its response to the sudden injection of fuel was instant. It careened forward and smashed into what was left of the burning hulk's front end. The wreck spun away as the TUPI rammed its way through.

"Where are we going, Jimmy?" Ilse called back to him.

"Turn right up here."

The intel officer swung hard on the wheel when she reached the right turn. The vehicle leaned hard to the left, its wide tires squealing in low protest.

Ilse glanced out of the side window and caught sight of the remaining TUPIs following her. She let out a sigh of relief and focused ahead—

Only to be hit by a truck that she didn't see.

The intel officer's shoulder and head hit the side window, sending pain shooting through her body, and her vision swimming like a whirlpool. She opened her mouth to speak but all that escaped her lips was a low moan.

Hawk fared no better. He cried out in pain as his side crashed into the unforgiving rim of the turret. Another rib broken and burning pain seared through his body. "Motherfu—"

"Bravo One, report," Anja's voice seemed far away as Hawk fought back the darkness of unconsciousness. "Bravo One, report, over."

"It hurts," he gasped.

"Say again."

Through his haze, Hawk caught movement from the truck that had hammered them. Two armed men climbed from the cab. Hawk grabbed for his SIG, pulling it free. "I said, it frigging hurts," he growled through gritted teeth, unleashing the whole of the handgun's magazine at the two men from the truck.

Both fell to the pavement with multiple gunshot wounds leaking copious amounts of blood.

Anger surged through Hawk as he reloaded. "Ilse, are you all right?"

"I'm still alive."

"Jimmy?"

"I'm here."

"Get this thing going," he called down.

The other vehicles were backed up behind them.

"It won't start."

"Bloody hell," Hawk fumed. "Alpha One, we're a lame duck. Coming to you."

"Roger that."

"Everybody out," Hawk ordered as he slid painfully from the turret. With each movement and breath, he felt as though someone was attacking him with a knife. He grabbed the G36 and climbed from the TUPI. Ilse noticed the way he moved and asked, "Are you alright?"

"Busted another rib."

"Damn it, Jake."

"Not my fault. Someone hit us with a bastard truck and—" He gasped and dropped to a knee.

"Jimmy, help me," Ilse ordered and rushed to Hawk's side.

They assisted him to his feet and ushered him to the next vehicle in the line. Anja climbed out and held the door open. "Get him in here before they catch up with us."

They got Hawk into the TUPI and Jimmy climbed in as well. Ilse said to Anja, I'll head back to Grizz and Nemo."

She hurried off and Anja climbed in beside Hawk. Banging on the driver's seat, she signaled that Elias was to get the vehicle moving forward once more. The Talon commander turned her gaze on Hawk. "Are you alright, Jake?"

"I wish people would stop asking me that. I'm fine. Nothing a beer won't fix."

"You look pale. I can see the pain in your eyes."

The TUPI bumped over a hole in the road and Hawk gasped as agony seared through his body. He strained to get a grin on his face and said to Anja, "I'm going to pass out."

———

"GET EVERYONE ON THE PLANE," Anja snapped. "Our package first."

Harvey ran across to where Hawk was still slumped in the TUPI. He called over his shoulder, "Nemo, give me a hand."

The pair got Hawk out of the vehicle and carried him to the Global 7500 whose turbines were already fired and their high-pitched scream climbing higher.

Behind them came Ilse who, despite of her own pain,

was helping Maya. They climbed the stairs and disappeared inside, Jimmy following in their wake.

Anja turned to Elias. "I'm sorry, Elias. If I'd have known—"

"No, say nothing. You got what you came for, be thankful. I wish you luck in your quest, Anja."

She gave the man a hug. "Thank you. Be safe."

"You, too."

The Talon commander turned away and ran towards the plane before taking the steps two at a time and through the doorway. As she made her way through the cabin, she checked on her people. They all looked a little worse for wear. Her main concern though was Jake.

She put her head into the cockpit where the two pilots waited. "Get us up. Is the flight plan filed?"

"Yes, ma'am," Greg Stevens the pilot replied with a nod. "Next stop, Texas."

Anja went back into the cabin and sat opposite Ilse and Maya. "How are you feeling, Maya?"

"Sore. Relieved." She rubbed her side where a bandage covered her recent surgical wound.

"You'll be back home in no time."

"Thank you—for everything."

"It's our job."

"Is—is Jake all right?"

Anja glanced along the cabin. It was a reflexive glance. "I'm sure he'll be fine. As they say, only the good die young. I have a feeling Jake will live for a long time yet."

Maya gave her a wan smile.

The Talon leader stared at Ilse. "How about you?"

"I've got a headache, sore shoulder from where that truck hit us. I have a feeling I'll be discovering painful patches for the next few days."

"I'm sure you will. We'll spend those days in Texas. Analyze what we've found and take it from there. I think the team could use the rest."

Ilse gave her boss a wry grin. "We're pretty banged up."

"Yes. Medusa, however, isn't going anywhere. In fact, I'm sure they will be looking for us."

# CHAPTER FIFTEEN

*Somewhere Over the Atlantic*

CHARLOTTE ALLARD'S phone was going berserk with incoming and outgoing calls across the globe. The French woman was white-hot with rage and trying to assuage it by finding the person or persons responsible for cleaning out her account. It rang once more, and she snatched at it. "Yes?"

"I might have something for you," the voice on the other end said.

"What is it going to cost me?"

"Ten million."

Charlotte chuckled.

"What is so funny?" asked the male voice.

"You, Joshka. You. Asking me for money to pay you for information. Money I don't have."

"I'm sure you will be able to get it, Charlotte."

She thought for a moment. Yes, she would be able to but she wasn't about to tell him that. "I might be able to scrape together a couple of million Euros."

"US dollars, Charlotte," Joshka replied.

"You might be lucky."

"And the painting," the man told her.

Charlotte hesitated. She knew what painting he referred to. It was a Picasso painted in 1901. "No, Joshka. It is worth more than fifty-million."

"Do you want to get your money back or what, Charlotte?"

The ultimatum did nothing to sooth her temper and she made a mental note that once her money was recovered, she would find a nice quiet hole to drop Joshka into. "All right, Joshka. We have a deal."

"Good. When can I expect you?"

"I will meet you in Paris in ten hours."

"Where?"

"The usual place."

It was Joshka's turn to chuckle. "I think that we should meet somewhere public, Charlotte. Let's say at Pierre's in fifteen hours. We can have dinner while we're there."

The Frenchwoman sighed. "Fine. I will see you there, Joshka."

The call disconnected and Charlotte took a sip from her champagne glass before taking her phone and punching another number. She waited until it was picked up, and said, "I need some money."

A pause.

"Twenty million."

Another pause.

"Yes, the usual place."

She disconnected the call and punched in the number to make one more.

———

A waiter stood behind the chair that he'd pulled out, waiting for Charlotte to be seated. Across from her the man known as Joshka was already seated and waiting.

"Would madam like something to drink?"

Charlotte pulled her hair back behind her right ear and looked at the waiter. "Please. Maybe a red?"

"Does madam have a choice?"

"Something expensive, Mister Fortier will be paying."

The waiter bowed slightly and said, "As madam wishes."

Moving away from the table he went to get the wine, making his way through the plush restaurant

"Well, what do you have?" Charlotte asked.

"You look rather lovely tonight, Charlotte," Joshka said.

She wore a blue form hugging dress with clear sequins scattered intermittently over it. Her long hair hung down her back, and the cut of her dress in front was so low as to expose the deep cleft of her cleavage. Her lips were a dark cherry red and her eyes had a minimalist makeup look with a fine liner and dark mascara. "Thank you."

"Who's the lucky lady?"

"Pardon?"

"Well, you didn't get dressed up like this just for me," he pointed out.

"If you must know, I'm off to see someone exotic after we finish here."

Joshka nodded. "Do you have the painting?"

"No. I've changed my mind. I'll give you the ten million you originally asked for."

He looked disappointed. "I thought—"

"Take it or leave it, Joshka," Charlotte said firmly.

He stared into her hard eyes, seeing no indication of any give, and knew it was futile. "All right. Ten."

Charlotte opened her purse and took out her phone. She dialed a number and then handed it to Joshka. "Give him the number and it'll be transferred."

He took the cell and waited. Reeled off a ten-digit number and then passed the cell back to Charlotte who put it away. Joshka then checked his own phone to make sure the money had been transferred. When it was done, he returned it to his pocket.

"What do you have?" Charlotte asked.

"You aren't the only one looking for this person. Viktor Medvedev also has a personal interest."

"No shit. What do you have?"

"They're a team working for Global based out of Hereford. Word is that the British government asked them to form a taskforce to take on Medusa. Apparently their first job was to find the girl that was taken from the—function you attended."

"Do you have names? Photos?" Charlotte asked, an excitement growing within, and her eyes revealing eagerness.

Joshka placed a folder on the table and pushed it towards her. "Everything you might require should be in there."

There was one more question on her lips. "Do you know where they are?"

"As a matter of fact, I do."

---

*Outside Galveston, Texas*

The team had been in Galveston for almost a week. Hawk had spent many of those days in hospital but had been discharged the day before. Now he lay back on a sofa in the accommodations provided for them by Eli Jones. It was a recently acquired vacant ranch, and with seven bedrooms, was ideal for the team's R & R.. There were three outbuildings, one of which was a large bunkhouse. Harvey and his team saw fit to utilize it for themselves. That left Anja, Ilse, Jimmy, and Hawk in the ranch house.

Hawk picked up the book he'd been reading. A World War Two non-fiction book about the SAS that he'd been given by Ilse on one of her visits while he was a patient.

"How is it?" she asked as she walked into the living room.

He looked up at her and smiled. "It's really quite good. Thanks for getting it."

"Couldn't have you getting too bored in the hospital. You'd have become a pest."

"Too late for that."

She smiled. "You said that, not me."

"How are you feeling after our sojourn?"

"Still a little sore."

"Yeah, I know all about that."

Ilse sat in the lounge chair opposite the sofa. Hawk gave her a wry smile. "This is ominous. You aren't some kind of shrink, are you? The head shed didn't hire you because you're a psych specialist too?"

"No, I'm nothing of the kind. I'm just a lowly intelligence officer."

"Thank God for that. You had me worried for a moment."

"I am curious about something, though," she said, looking around the large room.

"What's that?"

"Why did you become a soldier?"

Hawk opened his mouth to speak then stopped. He frowned then said, "You know, I'm not real sure. My grandfather was a soldier, his father too. My dad was a doctor. Instead of killing people he saved them. Mum was a nurse."

"I bet that went down well when you joined?"

"Like a lead balloon. The old guy wouldn't talk to me for a year. My mother didn't like it, but she accepted it. It wasn't until I was about to leave for my first Afghan deployment that my father reached out. I think I had my mother to thank for that."

"Were you SAS then?" Ilse asked him.

Hawk shook his head. "No, not until after that first deployment. I saw them in action when we were supporting a raid on a compound where a suspected bomb maker was holed up. I knew then that's what I wanted to do."

"And then the dark side," she said, her eyes widening, a grin splitting her lips.

"That was an eye-opening experience," Hawk told her. "Some of the shit I saw, the missions I was asked to do, it takes a special kind of someone to pull them off. I guess I had the right skillset, if not the right temperament."

"Hmm. I saw your file. Problem with authority much?"

"Only the ones who were dicks," he shot back at her a little too defensively. "Sorry."

Ilse shrugged. "How do we rate on your 'Dick Meter'?"

"I think you'll all do. Just don't tell the boss."

"Tell the boss what?" Anja asked as she walked into the living room.

She was wearing jeans and a T-shirt. Her hair was tied back in a ponytail, wet from her shower. Hawk winked at Ilse. "Don't tell her that I've fallen madly in love with her."

"I'm guessing that you'd be a man used to rejection by now, Jake. Is that correct?"

He winced. "Harsh. At least you could let a man down gently."

Ilse chuckled. "I think you make your own landing, Jake."

He sighed. "True."

"How are the ribs?" Anja asked.

"Still hurt but I'll survive. Thanks for caring."

The Talon commander smiled. "You're welcome."

"What do you have there?" Hawk asked nodding at the folder in her hands.

"Some things we've been able to dig up after the last operation."

"Great, something real to read," Hawk said putting the book down.

"Hey," said Ilse.

"Sorry, Geller," Hawk said. "Intel wins out every time. What do we have, Boss?"

"I'm crushed, Jake. After I saved your life and all."

"I'd come over there and wrap my grateful arms around you, but it hurts."

"Are we done?" Anja asked, raising an eyebrow and tapping her foot.

"You want a hug too?" Jake asked.

She rolled her eyes as she opened the folder. "Hardly."

Hawk and Ilse grinned at each other.

"First things first," Anja said. "The pictures you took."

"Yes?" said Hawk.

"Absolutely useless."

"Crap."

"What's crap?" Harvey asked as he entered the room.

"Jake's pictures," Ilse replied.

"I could have told you that. He's a Brit. Useless as titties on a bull."

"Pull your head in."

"Can we get back to this, please?" Anja asked, her voice rising testily.

"Ma'am."

"Ma'am."

The Talon commander tried her best to hide her smile. It was good that her team had gelled as quickly as they had. Her expectations had been exceeded in fact. "Now, back to the photos. I may have exaggerated when I said they were useless. Although you would never make a photographer, Jake."

"Fair's fair, ma'am. I was acting under extreme pressure at the time."

"I know, I was just pulling your leg. See, two can play that game."

"You just need a little more practice."

Anja passed out the photos making sure Hawk got the one of the French woman. "The first of the girls you captured was Canadian. Helen Dorset. Twenty-three, from Ontario Canada. From what we can gather she was picked up in Mexico City two weeks before the Auction."

"She was bought by one of the guys who were referred to as high rollers," Hawk explained. "Now she's in the wind."

Anja nodded. "I'm afraid so. We tried to trace her through money transfers, but it seems that after our little foray in the banking sector all of the accounts have been closed."

"Great."

"Miss Meyer," Ilse said, "I have a contact in Berlin who might be able to help out with that."

Anja nodded. "Try, Ilse. That would be good."

"What about the second girl?" Hawk asked.

"Yes, Amelia Davis. She is a native of Jamaica. She was also taken from Mexico City around the same time as Helen Dorset."

"She was bought by the French woman," Hawk stated. "The one I took a photo of without the mask."

"Yes. The picture you have. The woman is Charlotte Allard. She lives in Paris and as you can guess is a very wealthy woman."

"What does she do?" Harvey asked.

"She has her fingers in many pies but the one which made her the woman she is today is her deceased father's property development business."

"If we know where she is, then let's deploy and go get her," Harvey said.

"That is the plan," Anja replied. "Once we've all had time to recover."

"If you're talking about me," Hawk stated, "I'm ready to go."

"Another week at least, Jake. Plus, Mister MacBride needs the rest as well."

"What about that other thing?"

"By other thing I assume you're referring to Medvedev?"

Hawk nodded. "Yes, ma'am."

"We're still working on that. He'll eventually put his head above ground and when he does, we'll be there to chop it off."

Suddenly Jimmy appeared in the doorway to the living room. His face held an excited expression and his eyes seemed to be rolling in his head.

Harvey stared at him. "Shit, kid, how much of that juice have you had?"

"Juice?" Jimmy looked dumbfounded, knowing that he was the only "kid" in the room, but wasn't sure what Harvey was talking about.

"Yeah, that shit you kids drink that keeps you all frigging wired."

He appeared to think for a moment before coming back with, "That? Yes, that. Um, I'm not sure. Wow, but yeah, I think I'm starting to feel it. Maybe too much?"

Hawk looked at Anja who was less than impressed with the young tech. "If you have something to say, Jimmy, get it out. Then after, you and I will talk."

"Ah, yes, ma'am." He stood there waiting.

"Well?" Anja asked impatiently.

"Well, what?"

"Damn it, kid, what do you have?" Harvey growled.

"Oh, yes. I think I've found out who bought the Canadian girl. No, no, I *have* worked it out."

"Who?"

"Lars Akker."

"Shit!" Hawk exclaimed and slammed his fist down on the sofa.

"Did I say something wrong?" Jimmy asked, his face a mask of confusion.

"I can't believe I was that close to the bastard and never got the chance to put a bullet in his frigging head."

"You know him?"

"I owe him a death, kid. His."

"Why?"

"Long story. Do you know what hole he crawled out of?"

"No. Somewhere in Eastern Europe."

"Do yourself a favor, Jimmy," Hawk said. "Get off the juice."

He nodded. "Yes, sir. I also have a theory."

"We don't have time, Jimmy," Anja said.

It was Ilse who spoke up for the young man. "I think we should listen to what he has to say, Miss Meyer. Underneath all of that hyperactivity is a smart person."

The commander sighed. "All right, what is it?"

"All of these high-profile people who were at the Brazil auction, I think they're tied to Medusa somehow."

"Of course, they are," Hawk snapped. "They're buyers."

"Jake, give him a chance," Ilse said softly. "Go ahead, Jimmy."

"I figure that they're more than just buyers. I think that they are like branches of the same tree if you like."

"Jimmy, why would Medusa sell their own product to themselves?" Anja asked.

"That's not what I'm saying." He looked at Ilse as though pleading for help. "They're separate but the same."

"I don't understand," the commander said.

"I think I do," Ilse said. "I think Jimmy is saying that the high-profile buyers are the branches that keep the tree alive. If we prune them back, then Medusa will eventually shrivel and die. And maybe in the process it will draw Medvedev out into the open and we can finally get him."

"How many branches do we have?"

"According to Jake I can see five, possibly six. Two of which we have confirmed."

"One," Hawk said. "The French woman. Akker is only a theory at the moment."

"So we start with her," Anja said. "Meanwhile we continue our search for who the rest of these so-called branches are."

"I think we can count on more once we get started," Ilse replied.

Anja looked grim. "I'm certain we can."

"I have a question," Hawk said. "What do we do about the isotope? Every time we take one of these girls out of wherever they are, it'll just lead whoever is after them straight to us."

"I have some people at Global working on that," Ilse explained. "I'm waiting to hear back in the next day or so. It would be good if it was a simple matter of masking the signal."

"Let's hope so," Anja replied. She then looked at Hawk. "Jake, have Ilse get you everything she can about Charlotte Allard. Formulate a plan and then bring it to me."

"Yes, boss."

Anja's gaze turned on Jimmy. "Now, Mister Garcia. Come with me."

"Oh, crap."

The two left the room and Ilse climbed to her feet. Hawk looked at her. "Where are you going?"

"To make sure she doesn't eat him alive."

Hawk chuckled. "Yeah, good luck on that score."

# CHAPTER SIXTEEN

*Outside Galveston, Texas*

THEIR FIRST SIGN of trouble was a cut to the power followed by the phone signal. There were only two of the team up and alert at the time. Grizz Harvey and Nemo Kent. Both Linc and MacBride had turned in an hour before. When it first went, they looked at each other across the moonlit room. Harvey had been engrossed in a late-night movie which was reaching its climax. "Shit."

Nemo placed the book beside him and stared out the bunkhouse window. "Must be just us, Grizz. There're lights on in the main house."

Then those went out too.

Simultaneously, both men kicked into action. "Fuck!"

Their first instinct was to dive for the floor. It proved wise as one of the windows exploded in a shower of glass as a fusillade of gunfire ripped through it. Harvey reached for his sidearm and crawled across the floor to find cover. "Nemo! Are you alright?"

"Still in the fight, Grizz."

"Can you see anything?"

"No, still kissing the floor."

"Grizz! Grizz!"

Harvey rolled onto his back and through the moon-light could see Linc standing at the corner of the doorway which led into the bunk rooms. "Stay there, Linc."

"Here. Take this." He threw something towards Harvey which landed on the floor next to him. It was his body armor.

Harvey shrugged into it and when he was done, Linc had one more item for him. "Here!"

The big man reached out and caught the Bren2 before it touched the floor.

"What about me, you fucking moron?" Nemo shouted.

"You're expendable, Nemo."

"Screw you."

Harvey scrambled across to the window and peered out. He tried to count muzzle flashes, but they kept springing up anywhere. "Linc, check the back."

"On it, Grizz."

The big operator brought up his weapon and started firing into the darkness. Nemo joined him. "What I'd give for some night vision about now."

"Just start shooting. We'll worry about that later."

"Yeah, if we're still frigging alive."

Harvey's first magazine ran dry. "Changing!"

He replaced the empty with a fresh one and recom-menced what he was doing. Behind him in the doorway, Mac appeared. "Grizz, the pricks are out the back too."

"Roger that."

The big operator glanced at the ranch house and saw the flashes from that direction. They were going after the house as well. It was planned which meant they'd been under surveillance, and they'd missed it. "Damn it."

A bullet cracked as it flew past his head. He was searching for a target when he saw a flash. He immediately knew what it was and dived for the floor, taking Nemo with him. "Incoming!"

Then the world exploded.

─────

HAWK SHOOK ILSE AWAKE. "What is it?"

"Something's up," he whispered. "Get the boss."

As she climbed from her bed, she realized that he was dressed in his combat gear and carried his Bren2. He also had NVGs on his head. "Put this on," he said to her.

Ilse shrugged into her body armor and took a Bren2 he held out to her. Then the NVGs. "Take the comms as well."

Although her room was in semi-darkness there were other parts of the ranch house that remained illuminated. "Shouldn't we turn out the lights as well?"

"No. Whoever is out there will know we know. They'll cut the power before they come." He handed her another set of kit. "Here's the boss' gear."

"What are you going to do?"

"I'm going outside. You fort up in here. Got it?"

"Got it."

"It's an awfully big place to defend, Jake," Ilse pointed out.

"You'll be fine. Trust in yourself. Just don't give Garcia a damned gun."

"Roger that."

"Go now."

─────

HAWK SLIPPED out the rear door, his suppressed Bren2 up at his shoulder, his NVGs down. With him he carried another two sets. He figured to try and make it to the bunkhouse and get Harvey and one of his team out in the

192

wild with him. That was the theory anyway. As soon as he exited, he slipped into the garden which ran alongside the pool.

Crouching low, he walked along the rear of the house using a small hedge for cover. He thought that if he reached the corner of the house, he could skirt the pool and then make for the barn. From there it wasn't far to the bunkhouse.

Hawk froze when he saw the first movement. Someone was edging along the rear of the house. He saw them stop near something which was sticking out of the wall. The fuse box. They opened it, and just before cutting the power, Hawk heard the sound of gunfire rip across the yard. They were hitting the bunkhouse.

It was only a matter of heartbeats and the main ranch house followed. Then Hawk shot the intruder.

The man dropped where he stood. Hawk rushed across to him and knelt as the man choked out his last breath. The Brit searched him hurriedly, looking for any ID. He found nothing. Next, he reached for the man's comms. He put the earpiece next to his own ear and heard the chatter coming through. The bastards were speaking French.

He dropped the earpiece and came up into a crouch. "Bollocks."

From the front of the house Hawk could hear gunfire. It was intense; maybe too intense. He swept the approaches to the pool area, his laser sights turned off. The last thing he needed was for anyone with NVGs to be able to pinpoint his position by his own laser.

Breaking cover, Hawk had only gone a few paces when two shooters appeared. Just as he thought, concentrate the fire at the front and slip someone in the back. Hawk stroked the trigger on the Bren2 twice. The first shooter stumbled and fell. By the time he was face down on the sandstone pavers, Hawk had changed his aim and repeated the dose of violence. The audible impact of both rounds reached out to the Brit as the shooter followed his comrade to the ground.

"Alpha One, copy?"

"Copy, Jake."

"How are you faring?"

"We've got at least six shooters to the front of the house, over."

"You're three—"

Another shooter appeared and the Bren's charging handle rattled back and forth twice more.

"Make that four less out here, Alpha One. Proceeding to the bunkhouse, over."

"Roger that, Jake. Good luck."

Hawk skirted the pool and went down the stairs onto the grass, sweeping for threats as he went. Then came the explosion. An orange fire ball lifted into the night from the front of the bunkhouse. Hawk swore and dropped to a knee. He waited for a moment. The gunfire still reached out to him, a sign that someone was still in the fight for the bunkhouse.

Hawk hurried forward until he reached the barn. He moved along its back wall until he could see the attack coming in on the bunkhouse from the rear.

Stepping clear of the barn wall, he walked steadily forward, picking off targets as he went.

WHACK! WHACK! One down. Shift aim, WHACK! WHACK! A second shooter down. A third shooter suddenly realized something was wrong and spun on his heel. Through his own NVGs he saw Hawk coming towards him. Firing a hasty burst at the Brit, each round flew wide, digging into the ground around his target's feet.

"Fuck!" Hawk hissed, flicking the fire selector to auto on the Bren2 and squeezing the trigger.

The shooter did a macabre dance before falling backward, his weapon spilling from his grasp.

Hawk pushed forward stepping over the body.

Another figure loomed in front of him but soon disappeared as a burst of fire emanating from the bunkhouse sent them scurrying back into cover.

The Brit circled around until he could come up on the bunkhouse from the side. He was about to let his presence be known when a shadow reared up about twenty meters from where he stood, and a right arm went back and then forward.

Hawk hit the ground, burying his head under his arms. He felt the warmth of the grenade blast wash over him, his ears ringing. He looked up and saw two men advancing in his direction. *How many of these pricks were there?*

Whipping his Bren up, he was about to fire when another burst from the bunkhouse saved him the trouble. He waited to see if more shooters would appear. When they didn't, he called out, "Hey the bunkhouse! Grizz, you there?"

"Is that you, Jake?"

"Affirmative."

"Come on in."

Hawk got to his feet and ran for the back door. Once inside he was met by Linc. "What the hell are you doing out here?"

"Thought I might take a walk," Hawk replied changing out the magazine on the Bren. "Here."

Hawk gave him a set of NVGs and a comms link. "Where's Grizz?"

"At the front?"

The Brit made his way to the door. "Grizz, you still breathing?"

He could hear the bullets hammering the outside wall. What was left of it. The big operator emerged through the doorway and stood against the wall opposite Hawk. "What's going on? Are the others all right?"

"For the moment. Here." He tossed the NVGs and comms across the gap.

Harvey put them on. "Could have used these from the get-go."

"Feel like a midnight stroll amongst the daffodils?" Hawk asked.

The big man nodded and charged his weapon. "Yeah, let's give them some fucking fertilizer."

"Follow me."

"Nemo, hold the fort for a bit. I'll be right back," Harvey shouted around the corner of the doorway.

"Make it quick, Grizz, I'm getting low on ammo."

"Be right back."

They headed out the back which was now clear since Hawk had cleaned house. Linc followed them. Hawk said, "We'll clear the front of the bunkhouse and then push up to the ranch house."

"Roger that."

While the two team men went left, Hawk went right. They were hoping to flank the attacking force from both sides in a pincer. As soon as Hawk reached the front corner of the bunkhouse, he engaged his first target. The man fell into the lush grass at his feet, a cry of pain alerting his comrades of his passing.

Two of them turned their attention on the Brit, their automatic weapons spewing a fusillade of bullets which chewed splinters out of the wood structure. Hawk ducked back, allowing the heavy fire to dissipate before firing again. This time it was a longer burst and one shooter fell wounded beside his friend.

To Hawk's left, at the other end of the bunkhouse, firing erupted as Harvey and Linc emerged from the shadows. They worked together as a well-oiled machine, picking targets and killing them. Hawk pushed forward, his Bren adding to their firepower. The attackers were taken by surprise and on the backfoot.

The three Talon men pushed harder, ignoring the incoming rounds, relying on their training to keep them alive.

"Loading!" The call came from Linc. Harvey covered him as he switched magazines.

Hawk shot another attacker and their front seemed to be clear. He swept the ground before them left and right and found no more targets. He came to his feet and did a tactical reload as he walked past Harvey and Linc. "Let's get the rest of these bastards. Alpha One, we're on our way."

———

ILSE AND ANJA stood beside what was left of two large window frames, shattered by constant gunfire originating from several positions out near the turnaround. Jimmy was in a back room watching their rear, Anja figured it was the safest place for him plus he could give warning should more attackers gather out there.

Both women were bleeding. Anja from a small nick to her forehead by shattering glass from the window under the first heavy fusillade. Ilse's wound was a little more serious, a shallow furrow on the upper part of her left arm. Her sleeve was wet, but she ignored the burning pain as she sought another target through the green haze of the NVGs. A sudden shout from Anja made her blood run cold.

"*Last mag!*"

Ilse found another target and fired at it. The bullets hammered the area around the shooter until the magazine ran dry. The intel officer swore, wishing she'd had more practice with the Bren2. "Changing!"

Ilse ducked back out of sight until the weapon was ready to go again. Then she leaned back around and—
"Shit!"

A hailstorm of bullets hammered into the house, passing through the window. It covered the attacker's final push towards the building.

"I'm out!" cried Anja as she reached for her handgun.

Ilse was about to lean around the window opening to fire when a shooter burst through. He hit the floor, turning over, looking for a target. Ilse sprayed a long fusillade of bullets which hit the shooter as he was bringing his own weapon into play.

Three rounds hammered into his chest, hitting his body armor. The fourth ripped through his throat and put him down and out of the fight.

Opposite her, Anja was firing at another shooter who'd breached. Her handgun crashed three times, hitting the man in his chest. The body armor took the force of the rounds, which carried enough impact to disable the man who sank to his knees. With a shout, she changed her aim and shot him in the head.

The man flopped to the floor and never moved. She looked over at Ilse. "Frigging *arschloch*."

Then as suddenly as it had begun, the firing stopped and all was quiet.

"Coming in," a voice called out and they recognized it as Hawk.

"Come ahead," Ilse called back.

The three men entered and looked around through their NVGs. "You alright?" Hawk asked.

"Just," Anja replied.

"Where's Jimmy?"

"Out in the back room."

"I'll check on him," Linc said.

He'd only taken one step when they all heard a frightened whimper and the crunch of boots on debris. They all looked in the direction it came from and saw Jimmy, a fearful expression on his face, being pushed towards them by possibly the last remaining shooter holding a gun to

Jimmy's head. "Drop your weapons or I kill this sniveling wretch."

Hawk held up his left hand. "Whoa there, Frenchy. Let's think about this for a moment. Jimmy, are you alright?"

"I—"

"Shut up," the Frenchman snarled. "Do as I say."

"And then what?" Anja asked. "You'll walk out of here and let us all live?"

"No, there is the little matter of some money."

"Listen, cock," Hawk growled. "You're a little outnumbered here. I'm sure you can count. You're screwed either way. How about you put your gun down and we'll work something out."

"Jake," Jimmy blurted out.

"Take it easy, Jimmy, you'll be fine. I promise," Hawk said trying to ease the young man's fears. "What's it going to be, Frenchy. The second is the only option that gets you out of here alive."

The Frenchman paused briefly considering the choices. The gun in his hand crashed and the side of Jimmy's head exploded. The kid dropped to the floor amongst the detritus scattered across it.

"Motherfu—" The weapon in Hawk's hand chopped off the rest of his words as well as the cry from Ilse.

The Frenchman jerked and dropped to the floor beside the dead computer tech. Hawk rushed forward and crouched down beside Jimmy. "Oh, heck, kid, what did he do to you?"

The Brit rocked back and sat on the floor. He took his NVGs off and threw them across the room. *"Fuck!"*

———

Charlotte was woken from slumber by her cell vibrating across the polished top of her nightstand. The early morning sun was filtering through a gap in the heavy drapes, the rays reaching across the room, displaying a surfeit of dancing dust motes.

The French woman rolled over, her movements disturbing the ebony skinned beauty beside her. She fumbled with the phone, eventually finding the answer button. "Yes?"

"There's been a problem." It was a man's voice. Pierre, her security expert.

Charlotte knew the voice immediately. She sat up, wide awake, the covers dropping away from her chest. "What problem?"

"They are all dead."

"What do you mean, all?"

"All of them. The whole team."

"What? *Mon Dieu!*"

"What do you want done?"

Charlotte's mind whirled. The men who'd taken the job were meant to have been the best. Yet they were all killed.

"Miss Charlotte?"

The last of her loan was sunk into the venture. They were meant to get her money back. Now she would be forced to liquidate assets just to keep going. And that would take time. "Shit."

"Pardon?"

"Do nothing. Just observe them. I want to know where they go when they leave America."

"Do you think they will come to France?"

"Of course, they will, you fool," she snarled, checking to make sure her bed partner wasn't disturbed by her outburst.

"Then might I suggest that you find more men who might be able to—"

"And pay them with what?" she asked vehemently. "I will need to sell some assets just to get the money. And that will take time. You said—assured me that these men were more than capable of doing what was required."

"I assured you as I myself was assured, Miss Charlotte. But if you need funds, there is one person who may extend you a loan for a short period."

She knew who he was talking about. She also knew that they would ask the earth in interest. "I can't."

"Can you afford not to?"

"Possibly not."

Charlotte disconnected the call before punching in a new number. After two rings an automated voice asked, "Client ID?"

"Antionette seven-four-eight-six-one-one-two-five."

The line disconnected.

Two minutes later the cell rang. This time a human voice. "Client ID?"

Charlotte repeated the name and number.

"Is this call secure."

"Yes, it is."

"What can we do for you, Miss Allard?"

"I need funds."

"How much?"

"Fifty-million dollars."

There was a pause.

"Can you help?"

She heard the sigh from the other end. "I will have to confer with the boss."

"I understand."

"There will be a twenty-five percent fee, you understand?"

"Yes, Leonid, I understand."

"Give me a few minutes."

The call disconnected and Charlotte tossed the cell onto her bed. Seething, she stood then crossed to the twelve-foot double windows and drew back the curtains.

Sunlight flooded into the room bathing her naked body in a golden glow. The sky was cloudless, and she could feel the warmth of the sun's rays on her face. Closing her eyes momentarily, she enjoyed the feeling, blocking out her problems. When she opened them again, she looked out the window to see two of the four armed guards patrolling her estate grounds.

She heard the cell buzz and walked back to the bed. Charlotte picked it up and said, "Yes?"

"It's done. Fifty million for a twenty-five percent fee. It will be transferred to your account."

"No. I want it in cash, Leonid."

"All right. You can collect it in Berlin. I will arrange to meet you there in five days."

"Five days?" Her voice was pained.

"Or we can make it ten."

"Five will be fine. Thank you, Leonid."

"Mister Medvedev said the payment will be due in three weeks."

"Three weeks? After all of the business I do with him?"

"Three weeks, Charlotte, or he will welcome payment in other ways starting with your pleasure houses in Paris, Marseille, Strasbourg, Toulouse, Le Mans, and Nice. He has also heard about your art collection."

Charlotte ground her teeth together. "Fine."

"A pleasure as always, Charlotte."

"But you provide the security. One of your teams," she added.

There was a long silence.

"Did you hear me, Leonid?"

"I did, but now I am curious. Why the insistence of security? I thought Pierre took care of that for you?"

She couldn't tell him. If she did, he would take back the offer.

"Yes, or no?"

"We always have good security with face-to-face deals, Charlotte. Do not worry."

"Good," she grunted and disconnected.

# CHAPTER SEVENTEEN

*Galveston, Texas*

IT WAS RAINING the day they buried Jimmy Garcia. A special graveside service was held with only the team, Mary Thurston, Jimmy's parents, and the pastor in attendance. Hawk stood in stoic silence staring at the open grave with rivulets running down his face as though he was doing penance for letting the young computer tech get killed.

When the service was over, Thurston and Anja passed their condolences to Jimmy's parents before they left.

Ilse moved in beside Hawk and held a black umbrella over them both. "It's not your fault, Jake."

"Then why does it feel like it is?" he asked morosely.

"You can't carry that with you. He was a big boy; he knew from the start that this was going to be dangerous."

"He wasn't cut out for this life, Ilse. He should never have been there."

"And that rests on me," Thurston said as she stopped near them. "I was the one who ticked off on it. I should never have allowed it."

"I'm just as much to blame, Jake," Anja added. "I could tell from the start he wasn't going to fit. I hoped that he could be trained, but I dismissed that after the briefing when he told us about Akker. When I took him aside, I told him that he didn't belong."

"It's true, Jake," Ilse confirmed. "I was there."

Anja continued, "He was due to leave the morning after he was killed."

Jake was stunned. "Why didn't he say something?"

"He asked us not to until he was gone. He didn't want to look weak in your eyes."

"Shit, I wouldn't have judged him. This life isn't for everyone." He paused, then, "What do we do now? Are we going after that bitch?"

Anja nodded. "We leave this afternoon."

"For Paris?"

"No, Berlin."

"Why Berlin?"

"We have intel that Charlotte Allard will be meeting with Medvedev in Berlin."

"Medvedev? Our Medvedev? Why?"

"We're not sure," Thurston replied.

"How good is the intel?" Hawk asked.

"We're still vetting it," Thurston said truthfully.

"So, we could be walking into a shit storm?"

"You could very well be," Thurston confirmed.

Hawk stared at Anja. "You know how this guy works; what do you think?"

"It stinks."

"Yet you still want to go ahead and do it?"

"Yes."

"Then we're going to need a good plan."

"Yes, we are."

———

"I'm not sure you should be here, Viktor," Leonid said to his boss.

"Why don't you let me worry about that, Leonid," his boss replied.

"You are too exposed. It isn't necessary."

"For once, the mouse is right," Rogov said. "You have people for this."

"That's right, people who work for me and do as I say," Medvedev said testily. "Now, is everything in preparation?"

Leonid nodded. "Yes. The location was given to the right people and the trap will be set. But—"

"But what, Leonid?"

"Is it wise using one of our best buyers as bait?"

"I see no problem with it."

"Then shouldn't we at least tell her?"

"Like she told us of her operation on American soil?" There was sarcasm in Medvedev's voice. "Maybe if she had informed us what she'd intended then Kir and his team could have been deployed and the problem dealt with. No, we tell her nothing."

"Fine, but I still don't like the idea of you being so exposed. We have gotten this far without you doing it. For the last operation in Berlin it wasn't necessary, just as it isn't now."

"You sound like a nagging wife, Leonid. I grow weary of it." Medvedev turned his gaze on Rogov. "Are your people ready?"

"Yes."

"Good. All we have to do now is wait."

Medvedev rose from his chair and left the room. Leonid turned to Rogov. He despised the man but for the moment was the only ally he had. "You know this is a bad idea. I need you to put someone on him constantly. They may take the bait, but I'm thinking they are smarter than we give them credit for."

Rogov nodded. "I will see to it."

———

*Over Spain*

Studying the folder for the past four hours, Hawk gradually committed everything to memory. Charlotte Allard was staying at the Hotel Berlin, an upmarket place in the center of the city. According to intelligence, when she traveled, her head of security Pierre and two other bodyguards were with her almost constantly. The meeting was to be in the old warehouse district at ten. He looked at the pictures once more.

"Find anything we missed?" Ilse asked him as she sat down opposite.

"No, I just wish we knew what the other side were up to."

"Should we work out a plan?"

"I guess. How about we just drive in there and kill them all?"

"As much as that would bring me joy," Ilse replied, "we need someone alive to try and disassemble the network."

"Well, there might be another way, then."

"Enlighten me?"

"We take the French woman before the meeting."

Ilse frowned. "I don't think the boss would go for that."

"Get her up here and we'll run it past her."

The intel officer shrugged. "All right."

In under a minute Anya had joined the pair, and Hawk began giving a rundown of his plan. "I say me and

Grizz infiltrate the hotel, take out her minders and then use her to get close to Medvedev at the meeting."

"I'm listening, Jake," Anja said warily.

"That's it. Nothing else."

"What do you mean that's it?"

"That's it."

"I think you left out the part where you and John get killed," Anja replied.

"Do you have friends at Interpol?"

The Talon commander nodded. "Yes."

"How soon could you get a team together?"

"I don't know."

"They could be outside the perimeter on standby. Once we secure Medvedev, they can storm in and secure the site."

"It's the only way to do it if you want him alive. If we work from the outside in, he'll get away. My way we get the French woman and Medvedev. A good night's work if you ask me."

Anja thought about it long and hard. She looked at Ilse. "What do you think?"

"It's crazy but it could work."

Anja sighed resignedly. "All right, Jake, we'll do it your way. Just don't get yourself killed."

———

*Berlin, Germany*

"We've got two hours to get this right," Anja said over the comms to both men in the Black Mercedes. "If you screw this up here, it's all over."

"You worry too much," Hawk replied. "Simple job."

"Famous last words, Mister Hawk."

"At least I'll get some." He looked at Harvey. "I'm

beginning to think I picked the wrong guy for this. You stand out like dog's bollocks."

"Better than looking like them."

"Touché, my gorilla-sized friend."

"Let's do this."

"Alpha Two, this is Bravo One, can you confirm the location of the subject? Over."

"Confirm floor 5, room 531."

"Do we have eyes inside?"

"Affirmative, Bravo One. There are two guards outside the door in the hallway."

"Thanks, Alpha Two. We're going in."

"Roger. Good luck."

The pair exited the Mercedes and jogged across the street towards the hotel. Behind them, Nemo pulled the vehicle away from the curb and disappeared into the Berlin night.

Hawk and Harvey walked across the hotel turn around and hurried towards the main entrance. They walked past the valet and in through the automatic doors. Inside was air-conditioned and cool. The floor was tiled in pink granite and the lobby was well lit with white light. There were pink granite columns throughout the large space, with potted plants and sofas arranged in cozy settings for guests to relax. Tasteful art in muted tones were arranged under lighting on the walls, the overall effect being luxurious but comfortable.

The pair avoided the main reception counter and instead headed directly towards the elevators. Hawk pressed the button and turned around to scope the lobby. "You see anything?" he asked Harvey.

"Nothing out of the ordinary."

"How do you know what ordinary is?"

"Shit. Nothing to set my Spidey senses tingling."

Hawk smiled. "You have Spidey senses?"

"Shut up, Jake."

The doors to the elevator opened and they stepped inside, not surprised at the tones of classical muzak. Hawk pressed the button, the doors closed, and he felt the elevator begin its ascent. Within several moments, it stopped and the doors to the car slid open quietly, a soft chime indicating the floor. The pair stepped cautiously into the hallway, looking both ways before setting off to their left.

They approached the right turn ahead which would put them on the path with destiny.

"Cameras are down. All clear to proceed," Ilse's voice was clear in their ears.

Turning the corner, they took note of their targets outside the suite door. The pair readied themselves as the distance between the two parties diminished. Twenty feet, fifteen-ten— "Abort, abort."

"I told you this was the wrong bloody floor," Hawk growled at Harvey.

Taking the Brit's lead, he shot back with, "The next time, you find it, asshole."

As they walked past the two men, a maid appeared at the end of the hallway where there was another right turn. The two kept up their banter until they reached the maid and Hawk stopped her. "Miss, can you tell me what floor this is?"

"Fünf."

"Pardon."

She giggled. "Sorry, this is five."

Hawk slapped Harvey on the chest. "See, I told you we were on the wrong floor. Thank you, miss."

"That's all right. Can I show you the way?"

"No, it's fine. I'll do the navigating from here."

She gave them a smile, turned, and walked away. The two men pretended to maintain their argument for several more moments before Ilse's voice came back to them. "Clear."

The two Talon men turned and started walking back the way they'd come. However, when they drew level with the two guards, they moved with blinding speed. Hawk's hand chopped across the guard's throat, stunning him, making him lurch forward. He then whipped his arms up and into position, and using all his strength, broke the guard's neck.

Opposite him, Harvey's actions were almost identical. No mess or fuss.

Hawk went through his guard's pockets and found a key card. Straightening up, he looked at Harvey. "You good?"

"Go."

Hawk reached into his coat and took out his SIG. Retrieving a suppressor from the other pocket, he screwed it on. Utilizing the key card to open the door, he slipped into the room, Harvey coming behind him, dragging the bodies with him.

Not worrying about his friend, Hawk moved further into the suite. Drawn by the noise of the door opening, a man appeared and stared straight at the Brit. Hawk squeezed the trigger of the SIG twice and put him down, two rounds center mass. *Shit! There was only meant to be two.*

He swept left and then right—another one. One round in the head put him to sleep.

The only one left was the French woman. "Clear, Grizz."

"Where the fuck did these other two clowns come from?"

"No idea? Why don't we ask Miss Allard? Who are they?"

"*Ils sont amis.*"

"Cut the crap, sweetheart. I know you speak English. I must say I do like you in this black dress you're wearing. Minus the mask."

Her eyes widened. "You are him?"

Hawk shrugged. "Yeah, well."

"I should kill you now."

"Wouldn't do you any good. You've got nothing left to go to."

She looked confused. "Pardon?"

"Interpol is seizing everything you own as proceeds of crime. Seems like human trafficking doesn't pay after all."

He saw the flash of anger in her eyes. "You are police?"

"Something like that."

"I don't know how those men I hired failed to kill you," she snarled.

Hawk's expression hardened. "They got one. His name was Jimmy. Not much more than a kid."

She grunted. "What now? You shoot me as revenge?"

Harvey said, "As much as he wants to, lady, you're more useful to us alive than dead."

"What he says," Hawk said dryly.

"What do you want?"

"You have a meeting tonight, we're going with you," Hawk explained. "We're going to use you to get to Medvedev."

Charlotte laughed. "He's not going to be there. You waste your time."

"Our intel says different," Hawk replied.

"I will not help you."

Hawk stepped towards her, his anger reaching boiling point. He grabbed her throat with his left hand. The suppressor came up and touched the side of her head. "Listen, love, you've got two choices. Help us and you'll get a nice comfortable cell for the duration. You don't, I'll put a bullet in that pretty little head of yours. We've killed four of your people tonight, one more makes no difference to me."

She stared into his eyes seeing sparks of anger flashing

through them. But Hawk had to give her credit; if she was scared, she didn't let it show.

"All right, what do you want me to do?"

"Just be there and act normal. Once we make Medvedev, then we take him down."

"What if he doesn't come?"

"Then we'll still have you and it won't be a waste of a night."

"They will be expecting Pierre."

"Where is he?"

Charlotte nodded to the floor on her left. "There."

Hawk looked at the dead man on the carpet. "That could be an issue."

# CHAPTER EIGHTEEN

*Berlin, Germany*

"OUR MAN at the hotel says he saw these two enter." Leonid showed Rogov the pictures of Hawk and Harvey.

Rogov grunted.

Leonid stabbed his finger at the picture. "This man we know. He is the only one. Jacob Hawk, former British SAS. Very good at what he does. The other man is a mystery."

"It was not unexpected," the mercenary replied.

"No, but if they do something unexpected then it will cause us a lot of trouble."

"You worried about Viktor again?"

"I just wish he was in another damned country," Leonid growled. "What if they discover what we are up to and find out where Viktor is? We don't even know who leads them."

A knock was followed by the room door opening. A thin man entered holding a courier bag. "Sir, this arrived for you."

Leonid took the bag and waited for the man to leave

before he opened it to check the contents. When he did his fears grew exponentially. "Good God, no."

"What is it?" Rogov asked.

Leonid flicked through the pictures that were inside, coming back to the one on top. He picked it up and passed it to Rogov. "It seems an old friend has come back to haunt us."

"Who is she?"

"Anja Meyer. Former German Federal Intelligence. We've crossed paths before."

"At least you know who you're after now."

"Yes, and I know where she is," Leonid said holding up a piece of paper.

"Where?"

"She's at an Interpol safehouse here in Berlin. It seems that they brought in reinforcements for their special evening."

"Then we change the plan," Rogov said. "We go after them there."

"What about the others?" Leonid asked.

"We can arrange something for them too."

"I will inform Viktor."

Rogov looked at his watch. "We need to move now. We only have an hour."

"Gather your team and be ready."

———

"SITREP, BRAVO ONE," Anja asked as she looked over the multiple screens before her.

"All is quiet so far, ma'am," Hawk reported. "Any issues at the hotel?"

"None. The Interpol team is taking care of it." Anja looked at her watch. They were five minutes short of the designated time. "Alpha Two, status on the assault teams?"

Ilse was coordinating in the field. She was with Harvey's three men while the Interpol team was under the control of a Dutchman, Adam Klerk. Anja was at the safe-house with the rest of Interpol's Special Projects team under the command of Evert Martens.

"Alpha One, this is Alpha Two. Assault teams are ready."

"Copy. Standby."

She turned to Martens. "Now we wait."

The thin, red-haired man nodded. "That is the worst part. We have been after Viktor Medvedev for too long. And to learn that he is behind the global trafficking ring is a bonus indeed. But you have your own reasons for wanting him gone."

Anja nodded. "Yes." She looked at her watch. "All teams, standby. Target should be arriving at any moment now."

"I have a vehicle approaching," one of the Interpol team called from his station.

"Bring it up."

One of the four screens changed and a picture from the satellite feed appeared. It looked to be an SUV.

"All teams standby, we've got a vehicle approaching the rendezvous point. Snipers ready?"

"Affirmative."

"Vehicle should be coming into view...now."

———

"WE'VE GOT IT," Hawk said into his comms as the SUV swung into view. "All teams hold until I give the word."

"Copy, Bravo One," Ilse said over the comms. "You have control."

Hawk and Harvey climbed from the vehicle they were in and waited for the SUV to stop. "Alpha One, sitrep?"

"Looks all clear, Jake. Nothing on ISR."

The SUV sat immobile with its lights still on. A few moments later a figure climbed out and moved to the back of the car to retrieve a briefcase. From there the figure walked to the front of the SUV and stood in front of the headlights.

"Get her out, Grizz," Hawk said to Harvey. "Alpha Two, I have eyes on one X-Ray from the SUV, confirm."

"Confirm, Jake. I see no sign of anyone else at this time."

"Alpha One."

"Confirm, Bravo One."

Harvey brought Charlotte forward. "All right, walk over there, take the case, and confirm that Medvedev is here."

Her head snapped around. "Something is wrong."

"What is wrong?" Hawk asked.

"There is only one man. When I set the meeting, I asked for them to supply security because I was worried about you turning up here."

Hawk said, "Alpha One, confirm last report."

"Affirmative, Bravo One. What seems to be the problem?"

"Our guest of honor seems to think Medvedev is up to something."

"The screen is clear, Bravo One."

"What about the vehicle?"

"Three heat signatures inside."

"Copy." He turned to Charlotte. "We're clear, move."

"Something is wrong, I tell you," the French woman hissed.

"Just get moving."

Reluctantly Charlotte walked towards the man with the briefcase. "A mite skittish, isn't she," Harvey said in a low voice.

"She should have thought of that before she decided to lay down with snakes."

Harvey snorted. "I see what you did there."

"It's part of my undeniable charm," Hawk replied dryly.

They watched on as Charlotte reached the man with the case. There was a short discussion before Charlotte suddenly whirled, her mouth open.

"Something is—" Hawk never finished the statement before the French woman disappeared in a fiery blast which shook the warehouse district and blew both men backward into darkness.

———

ANJA FLINCHED in horror as the two people disappeared before her eyes. "Shit! Bravo One, report!"

No reply.

"Bravo One, report."

Static.

"Jake, report."

Only more static before. "Alpha One, Alpha Two. Bravo One and Two are down. I say again, Bravo One and Two are down."

"God, no. Not again," Anja moaned. "Ilse, report."

The comms crackled and the Talon commander only picked up every fourth or fifth word. "Say again, Alpha Two."

The comms went quiet. Anja turned to Martens. "Anything?"

The Interpol man shook his head. "I can't even raise my own men. It's almost like they're being jammed."

"No, no, not again. Ilse, talk to me."

Still just static.

Anja was growing more concerned and opened her mouth to try again when the safehouse was rocked by an explosion. Shouts of alarm were followed by several moments of panic as the sound of gunfire filled the air.

Anja grabbed for her SIG and turned in time to be hit with the blast of a concussion grenade. She dropped her weapon, her hands going to her ears. Staggering, she dropped to her knees.

Trying to clear the fog, she blinked her eyes and shook her head,. Anja looked to her left and saw Martens standing, falling as bullets punched into his chest. The sound of the firing sounded as though it was miles away through the savage ringing in her ears. Anja looked around, noting the bodies on the ground through the haze. She fumbled around on the floor, searching for her weapon, her movements uncoordinated and ungainly.

A movement in front of Anja made her stop. Looking up, she watched as the figure drew closer. As though in a dream, she narrowed her eyes, trying to make out the face.

"Hello, Anja."

The voice was distant.

"It has been a while."

Anja shook her head and squinted again. The face became clearer, then a wave of recognition of the man standing before her. "Viktor."

Medvedev grinned coldly. "Yes, it's me."

Anja tried to stand but couldn't. "I—I'll kill you."

"Yes, you have me afraid."

Anja snarled as she tried to gain her feet once more. She got her right foot under her and then pushed herself up, a growl of rage driving her. She staggered but steadied herself and stood erect before the people trafficker. Her nostrils flared as she drew in deep breaths and expelled them again.

Medvedev nodded appreciatively. "I admire your tenacity, my dear, but I'm afraid it has been all for nothing.

Then he shot her twice in the chest.

———

"JAKE, ARE YOU ALRIGHT?" Ilse. Her voice seemed far away. "Come on, Jake, talk to me."

His eyes fluttered open. "What happened?"

"Thank God. An explosion. We think the case was rigged."

"Shit," he groaned as he sat up. "Charlotte?"

"Gone. But that's not all. We have to go."

"Why?"

"It was a trap. We can't get through to the safehouse."

"Help me up."

Once on his feet, Hawk looked around at the scene. "Where's Grizz?"

"Over here, bonehead."

Hawk turned in the direction of the voice and saw Linc working on him. "What happened to you?"

"Dislocated my shoulder when the blast knocked me over," the big man explained.

"We have to go, Jake," Ilse said.

Hawk held the palm of his right hand to his head as a jolt of pain went through it. "All right, I'm coming."

He started to follow her and stopped near MacBride. He pointed at the Bren2. "You mind?"

The operator shook his head. "Not in the least."

He passed the Brit his weapon and a spare magazine. "Keep your head down, Jake."

"Nemo," said Harvey, "go with him."

"Roger that, Grizz."

They hurried back to one of the SUVs which had been supplied by Interpol for their use while in country. Hawk climbed in the passenger side, leaving the uninjured Ilse to do the driving; Nemo took the back seat. Twenty minutes found them arriving at the safehouse which was engulfed in flashing lights from police and emergency vehicles. "Oh, no," Ilse breathed. "We're too late."

"Leave the heavy artillery in the vehicle," Hawk said to Nemo.

They tumbled from the SUV and hurried towards the cordoned perimeter. They were stopped by a police officer. "We need to get in there," Ilse said.

"You cannot go any further. It is a crime scene."

She showed him her credentials and said, "We work with Interpol. Our boss is in there."

He stared at them for a moment and said, "Wait here."

He disappeared for a moment and came back with his commander. "Who are you?"

"My name is Ilse Geller. We are working with Interpol. We were on an operation when we lost contact with our command structure."

"Yes, well, if you saw inside, you would understand why."

"Are they all dead?" Hawk asked.

"There was one survivor. Although I'm not sure how long they will be alive for."

"Was it a woman?" Ilse asked.

"I'm not sure."

"Can you find out?"

He sighed. "Give me a moment."

He spoke into his radio for a moment and when he was finished the expression on Ilse's face told Hawk what he needed to know.

"It was a woman," the officer replied. "According to her ID her name was Anja Meyer."

"Where have they taken her?"

"To the hospital, of course. But I'm afraid you are not going anywhere. Not until I get some answers about what the hell happened here."

———

THE MAN'S name was Schmidt. He was in overall command of the scene and had many questions for them to answer. Nemo stayed with the SUV while Schmidt took them inside to see for themselves what had happened. The place was a mess. The door at the front had been blown off on entry. There were bullet holes in the walls and bloodstains on the floors. Most of the dead had been taken away, however, some remained. "Seven dead in total," Schmidt said. "Only your friend remained alive. She had been shot twice in the chest."

"Any idea who did this?" Hawk asked already knowing the answer.

"I'm sure you will be able to fill in the missing pieces, Mister Hawk. Even you, Miss Geller. Shall we start with the explosion at the warehouse district earlier? It doesn't take a genius to put two and two together."

Ilse told him what had happened and why they were in Berlin. Schmidt shook his head. "I'm afraid this is going to be a very long night, Miss Geller. For all of us."

"Who is in charge here?" an authoritative voice called out.

Hawk saw Ilse pull a face before Schmidt said, "I am."

"My name is Berger. National Security Service. I need all of your people out of here until we are done with it."

Hawk looked at Ilse and whispered, "You know this guy?"

She nodded. "He's an A-grade asshole. He's the one who got Anja fired."

"So he's the one?"

"Yes."

"Who are you?" Berger growled.

Ilse lifted her head.

"You? What are you doing here?"

It was Hawk who answered. "We're on fucking holi-day. What are you doing here?"

Berger glared at Hawk but wouldn't be deterred from Ilse. "I asked you a question."

"We're working on an operation with Interpol," she replied.

"Not in this country you aren't."

"Just ease up, Adolf," Hawk said firmly.

"What did you call me?" Berger's temper snapped. He stepped forward and gave Hawk a shove. "What did you fucking call me?"

The intelligence man tried to follow up with his shove but the Brit was expecting it. Before Berger knew what was happening, he was on the ground face down with a knee in the middle of his back. "Listen up, you pretentious prick. I'm not someone you can push around, all right? Maybe I was a little out of line in calling you what I did, but if you keep following the track you're on, I'm going to kick you in the bollocks until they start ringing like fucking Big Ben, understand?"

Hawk felt Ilse's hand on his shoulder. "Let him up, Jake."

The Brit removed his knee and allowed Berger to make the undignified climb to his feet. He was beyond angry as was expected and directed it back at Hawk. "You're done in this country. I'll see you locked up for good."

Hawk took another step toward him. Ilse edged between them and said, "Jake, go for a walk. I can take care of this."

Hawk never moved.

She could feel his bunched muscles through his shirt. He was like a coiled spring about to explode. "Jake, look at me."

He kept his granite hard stare on the intelligence officer.

"Jake?"

He dropped his gaze, looking into Ilse's eyes.

"I've got this."

Hawk nodded abruptly. "All right."

He turned and stalked off.

"What kind of frigging animal have you got there, Ilse?" Berger snarled.

"Just shut the fuck up, Wolfgang, and listen. Maybe you might learn something."

———

HAWK WAITED OUTSIDE until Ilse was done. When she emerged, he asked her if she was all right. "I'm fine," she replied curtly.

"You sure?"

"Yes."

"I'm detecting a little hostility here."

She whirled on him, her eyes ablaze. "You ever do something like that again, I'll kick *you* in the bollocks until they sound like fucking Big Ben, understood?"

"What are you pissed at me for?" Hawk asked bemused. "The shit asked for it."

"Understand this, Jake, while Anja is out of action, I'm your boss. What I say goes, all right?"

Hawk suddenly felt like a reprimanded school kid. But she was right, and he knew he'd gone too far. "I'm sorry. It won't happen again."

"It better not."

"Where do we go from here?"

"The hospital."

———

IT WAS four hours before they received any news about Anja. The six of them remained in the waiting room for the duration, hoping and praying that the next snippet of news would be good. A doctor in green scrubs walked through a set of double doors and Ilse immediately came to her feet, Hawk stepping up alongside her. On one of the chairs, Nemo was asleep but a solid nudge from Linc brought him awake.

"Are you here for Miss Meyer?" the tired looking surgeon asked in heavily-accented English.

Ilse nodded. "Yes, how is she?"

"Do you know if she has any family?"

The question caused Ilse to swallow hard. "N—no, she has no one. Why?"

"We've done everything that we can, repaired the damage caused by the bullets, but now, the rest is up to her."

"What are her chances?" Hawk asked.

A pained expression came across his face as though he didn't want to hazard a guess. "Not good. Twenty percent chance of getting through the next twenty-four hours."

Ilse gasped.

The doctor continued. "If she gets past that, her chances increase, but not astronomically. I can tell you that the first twenty-four are critical."

"Can we see her?" Ilse asked.

"I'd rather you didn't."

She nodded. "If I leave my number with you, can you call if anything changes?"

"Yes. I'll let the ICU nurses know."

"Thank you, Doctor."

He gave them a grim smile and went back the way he'd come.

"I have to tell Mary," Ilse said.

"We need a place to get set up again," Hawk said.

"For what?"

"This thing isn't over yet," Hawk pointed out. "We need to find these bastards and put them in the ground."

"Jake, we just can't go off on some vengeance rampage. Viktor Medvedev will see us coming from a mile away.

He's one of the most capable, devious world criminals that I've ever come across. We need to do this the right way, or we end up in there like Anja or in the ground like Jimmy."

"Then what do we do?"

"I'll make some calls."

# CHAPTER NINETEEN

*Berlin, Germany*

"KARL, this is Jake; he's part of the new team I'm with under Miss Meyer," Ilse said to the tall, dark-haired man with black-framed glasses.

Karl Wolff pulled them down his nose, staring over the top of them at Hawk. "I see. I thought you were coming on your own."

"We need your help, Karl."

"All right, come in." He stepped aside and let them in through the front door of the terrace house. "Along the hallway and the first doorway on your left."

The living room was sparsely furnished as one would expect from a bachelor. However, it was so neat and tidy it spoke volumes to the man's OCD. "Sit down."

Hawk sat in a plastic covered lounge chair which crackled when he moved. He glanced at Ilse who gave him a 'don't say a damned word' look.

"What can I do for you, Ilse?" Karl asked.

"Like I said, I need your help. No doubt you heard about what happened last night at the warehouse district and then again at the Interpol safehouse?"

Karl nodded. "Yes—"

He stopped abruptly, his thoughts reeling as he tugged the pieces together in his mind. "You were there?"

"At the warehouse district. What have you been told?"

"Just that there was an explosion—something about an Interpol operation."

"That explosion killed Charlotte Allard," Ilse told him. "We were using her to get to Viktor Medvedev."

Karl's eyes widened. "He's here?"

"Yes."

"Shit, Berger will have a foal."

"He already had that. Last night when I saw him at the safehouse."

"I see—no, I wish I did see."

"How come you don't know this stuff already?" Hawk asked. "I thought you worked with the Intelligence Service."

"Not for much longer, I'm afraid," Karl said in a low voice.

"What happened?" Ilse asked him.

"My OCD."

"I thought that was under control?"

"It is, mostly, but Berger is using it to push me out. He's been slowly weeding out those of us who were on Anja's team when Valkyrie went sideways. Who are you working for, anyway? Interpol?"

Ilse shook her head and told him.

"Miss Meyer is with you?"

"Not exactly. She was shot last night when the raid went down on the Interpol safehouse. She's in hospital."

"She's going to be fine, right?" Karl asked, his tone hopeful.

"We don't know."

"What do you need me to do, Ilse. Whatever it is, count me in."

"How are your computer skills?"

"Just as good as they ever were."

"Then that's why I'm here."

"Let me just get my machine and I'll be right back."

He hurried out of the room and Hawk looked at Ilse. "Are you sure he's the right guy to help us?"

She stared at him. "Why? Because of his OCD?"

Hawk winced, she made it sound ugly. "Well...yeah, kind of."

"Oh, Jake," Ilse growled, the exasperation in her voice front and center. "That man used to be one of the best field agents the Service had. Right up until he was captured by a Russian oligarch who tortured him for a week before he was found. He spent time in hospital and came out the other side in one piece. Or so it was thought. His OCD appeared a month later. Berger was all set to throw him out as a liability."

"If it hadn't been for Miss Meyer, I would have been," Karl said, picking up on the conversation as he entered the room.

Hawk suddenly felt uncomfortable. "I—I'm sorry, Karl. I—"

"It's all right. I get used to people talking behind my back. Miss Meyer gave me the chance I needed. She knew I had good computer skills and could run the assault teams. She took that chance, and I was able to reward her for it."

Hawk felt like crawling into a hole and hiding for a week. "I'm sorry, Karl."

"Now that's out of the way, how about we get down to business?"

Ilse winced. "Karl, there is one more thing..."

He looked up from his screen. "Sure."

———

"PLEASE DON'T TOUCH THAT," Karl said to Nemo Kent who had picked up a small glass figurine of an angel. "I only cleaned it yesterday."

"Put it down, Nemo," Harvey growled.

"It's pretty."

"No, no, no," Karl said as he came out of his plastic covered lounge chair. "Not that."

He relieved Mac MacBride's hands of a replica Fabergé egg and put it back on the shelf exactly where it had come from.

"Will you all stop touching things," Ilse growled. "You're like bloody kids in a candy shop."

"He's got nice things," Nemo said innocently.

"I'd like to keep them that way, if possible," Karl said as he sat back down.

"Stand down, you clowns," Harvey snapped. "Let the man work."

Linc glared at them.

The only one who hadn't moved was Hawk. For the past hour he'd remained unmoving in the same position, his face impassive. Ilse looked at him and walked to where he sat. "Are you alright?"

He looked up at her as though coming out of a trance. "I'm fine, just waiting to see if your man can come up with something."

"He will. Don't—"

"Got it."

All eyes converged on the German intel officer. "What do you have, Karl?"

"An Ilyushin took off thirty minutes ago for Smolensk, Russia."

Hawk sat forward in his seat. "That could be anything."

"Yes, perhaps, but there was security footage of the plane on the apron. Someone got careless. And while we never got a picture of Medvedev, we did get these two."

A picture flashed up on the computer screen. "Meet Kir Rogov and Leonid Fedorov. Rogov is a mercenary for hire. Savage beast that one. Wanted across the globe by more than one law enforcement agency. His team are just like their commander. We received unconfirmed reports only recently of a small village in Mali being wiped out by white mercenaries. I'd put money on it being him."

"What about the other scouser?" Hawk asked.

It was Ilse who spoke. "Leonid is another who used to be FSB. He was recruited by Medvedev to oversee things for him. Don't let his looks deceive. This thin, wiry looking rat-faced man is good at what he does. He's a killer who didn't get to where he is by playing nice. If anyone knows the ins and outs of Medvedev's operation, it's him."

"Would Medvedev be traveling with him?"

"It's possible."

"Then that's where we need to be. Good man, Karl."

"I can't authorize an operation onto Russian soil, Jake," Ilse said. "That's up to Anja."

"I'm not talking about a full operation. Just send me."

"Whoa, Jake, think about what you're suggesting," Harvey said. "You need my team as backup."

Hawk shook his head. "You're no good, Grizz. Mac still needs recovery time and a walk in the woods won't do him any good. And three are more likely to be seen than one."

"I still can't authorize it, Jake," Ilse said. "It's up to Anja, and she's out of it."

"Then go to Thurston."

"Jake—"

"We have a chance to do something here before Medvedev turns into a ghost again."

Ilse stared at him, her thoughts turning over in her mind. She nodded. "Tell me what you have planned."

"Once we know where they're going you drop me in. I'll make a bit of trouble and see if I can get Medvedev."

"What do you mean by get, Jake?"

"I'm going to double-tap the bastard, that's what I mean."

"Just like that? You make it sound so...simple."

"Sometimes the simple plans are often the best."

"We'll see. I'll talk to Thurston and await her opinion. Until then, all of you get some rest. We could—"

"Wait," Karl said, cutting her off.

"What is it, Karl?" Ilse asked, seeing the panic on his face.

"You—you're not thinking of staying here, are you?"

The intel officer's face softened. "We've got nowhere else to go, Karl. I promise I will keep them under control."

Nemo walked out of the kitchen with an open milk bottle in his hand. "I think your milk is off, Karl. It tastes like shit."

Ilse closed her eyes and shook her head. "Give me strength."

———

"GOOD NEWS," Ilse said to Hawk after disconnecting the call. "Anja is faring better but she's not out of the woods yet."

"That is good. What did Thurston say?"

"She said yes. We move the team to Orsha in Belarus in two days. The German intelligence service has an operations center there we can use."

"How do they get away with that?" Hawk asked.

"Money, of course."

"The almighty dollar."

"You should know, I'm taking Karl with us."

"Are you sure?" Hawk asked.

"We need him now that Jimmy is gone. And the good part is, he knows how to use a weapon and has a lot of field experience."

"And he has OCD."

"Which he has under control, Jake. Give him a chance. Everyone on this team would not be here if they weren't given a second chance. Including you. Remember that."

"All right, give him a shot."

"Now that's out of the way, he wants to see us."

"Fine," said Jake. "Let's go and put some more condensation rings on his coffee table."

Ilse jammed her elbow into his ribs. Hawk buckled at the waist. Although his ribs were pretty much healed, they were still tender. "What was that for?"

"Just a reminder of what to expect if you keep up with the attitude."

"There was no attitude," he protested.

"Just shut up and follow me."

Karl saw them coming and smiled nervously. Hawk held up his hand. "Just relax, Karl. It's all good."

The intelligence officer sighed and placed a Glock 19 on the desk next to his computer. "That's a relief."

The Brit raised his eyebrows and glanced at Ilse who grinned at him. Hawk shrugged and turned his gaze back to Karl. "What have you got?"

"I managed to trace our persons of interest to an old munitions factory outside of Smolensk. It has been abandoned since the early nineties. Just the place for a weapons- and people-smuggler to set up base."

"Do you think he keeps the girls there?" Ilse asked hopefully.

"No. There's not enough heat signature activity to suggest it. There's maybe twenty people there at most. If he were keeping girls there, the signature would be off the scale."

"So what is he keeping there?" Hawk asked.

"Arms, most likely."

"Good, more bang for our buck."

"There was something else that I thought interesting," Karl said and brought up a picture on the computer. It was of a man wearing a wide-brimmed hat so that his face couldn't be seen. To Hawk it looked to be a deliberate ploy. Karl continued, "I ran some numbers through the system and going on height and build there is an eighty percent chance that this is Viktor Medvedev. If it is, he's not going to stay there long. My guess would be twenty-four to forty-eight hours."

Hawk was impressed. This guy, despite of his issues, seemed quite good at what he did. "We need to bring it all forward."

"Is there a problem?" Harvey asked as he walked into the room. His left arm was in a sling because of his shoulder.

"We've found Medvedev—Karl found him. He's outside of Smolensk."

"That's good news."

"Even better, Thurston ticked off on the operation."

"That's not so good."

Hawk patted him on the sore arm causing him to flinch with the pain. "Cheer up, Big Man, here for a good time, not a long one."

"When are we leaving?"

"Yesterday," Ilse replied. "Get everyone ready."

"Yes, ma'am."

Once the two men left the room, Ilse turned to Karl. "I need you, Karl."

He was surprised. "You—you want me to come with you?"

She nodded. "Uh, huh. You're the best at what you do. You just proved that. We can use you."

"I can't, I'm sorry, Ilse. I can't."

"Not even for Miss Meyer? She gave you a chance when no one else would. It's time to pay her back."

Karl nodded, contemplating the logistics. "Fine, I'll do it. But no more."

"Thanks, Karl."

———

THE MACHINE WAS BREATHING for her and sounded as though the hospital room was occupied by Darth Vader. The heart monitor showed the peaks of the steady heart rhythm. Ilse reached out and touched the comatose woman's hand. "I have to go away with the team. We've got a lead on Viktor we need to follow. Hopefully when you wake up, I'll have good news."

In a way she was hoping that Anja would wake, look at her, and give her blessing, saying to go do her best. But that wasn't going to happen. "Anyway, the others are waiting. I'll see you when I get back."

She was about to let go when Anja's hand gripped tighter and then the pressure eased. Ilse frowned and then smiled. Everything was going to be fine. She released her boss' hand and walked out of the room. Behind her, as she lay on the bed, Anja's eyes started to flutter open.

# CHAPTER TWENTY

*Old Smolensk Munitions Complex, 20km From the City*

"BRAVO ONE IS DOWN and proceeding towards target, over."

"Reading you loud and clear, Bravo One. The helo for extraction is in position and ready when you are. We have you on ISR. Good luck."

Hawk consulted his GPS and got a bearing on which direction he needed to travel. His current position was two klicks from the complex. He checked his gear: a Bren2, his SIG, four grenades, two flash bangs, extra ammo, and some bricks of explosive compound along with detonators and timers. He also had the benefit of night vision and the satellite feed which was beaming back to the safehouse.

The HALO (High Altitude Low Opening) jump had gone off without a hitch, the landing, he'd had better but was still in one piece so it was all good. He switched his laser sights on and pointed himself towards the complex. Time to earn his keep.

The forest he navigated was dark and damp. Late in the day had seen a storm go through the region. Two hours of careful going found Hawk on the outskirts of the complex.

"Alpha One, this is Bravo One. I've reached the target, over."

"Roger, Bravo One. Confirm you've reached target. Tell me what you see, over."

"The bonus is that the place isn't fenced. But they do have two search lights in towers."

"Roger, that corresponds with what we're seeing."

"Jake, this is Karl."

"Go ahead."

"Be aware that there is a Russian military base five klicks from where you are. Once this kicks off, you'll have a limited amount of time to get out."

"What's the ETA of the helo once it is up?"

"Ten minutes."

"I can work with that. Out."

Hawk moved forward out of the tree line. He was halfway across the open ground when the right search light started to sweep back across the area. He went to ground, remained still until it passed over him. Hawk came back to his feet and hurried forward until he reached the tower. He stopped and took out the first of the explosive bricks. A minute later it was set and ready to go.

The Brit raised his weapon and swept the area. Finding it clear, he moved along the perimeter, using the old buildings for cover.

"Jake, hold," Ilse said over the comms.

He dropped flat to the ground, unmoving. Ilse's voice came to him. It was calm, steady. "There is an X-Ray coming up on your right. His path will take him right on top of you, Jake. You'll need to deal with him."

"How far?" he whispered.

"Thirty feet."

Hawk let go of the Bren and grabbed hold of his

suppressed SIG. He eased it from the holster and said, "Give me real time, Alpha One."

"Twenty feet coming up on your four o'clock."

Hawk slowed his breathing and tensed himself. He could hear the guard's approach now as his feet swished through the grass.

"Fifteen feet."

Hawk rolled, bringing up the handgun. He fired twice at the surprised guard and saw the man fall. The Brit remained motionless for a moment before saying, "Sitrep, Alpha Two."

"It looks all clear, Jake," Karl said.

Hawk came to his feet and picked up the dead guard's weapon. He then dragged him across the damp grass into the shadows of a building where he left him. "Bravo One is Charlie Mike."

"Roger, Bravo One, you're continuing mission."

Grass gave way to asphalt sprinkled with weeds growing through multiple cracks. Hawk moved cat-footed until he reached the corner of another rundown building where he paused. "Alpha Two, how are we looking, over?"

"All clear, Jake."

Hawk left the security of the shadows, keeping low until he reached the second tower. He placed the explosives and set them, saying into his comms, "We're set here, I'm moving in."

"Jake, the biggest concentration of heat I'm seeing is towards the center of the complex in what looks like a double story building. You've also got two more guards which you might want to dispatch before things go loud."

"Copy. Where are they?"

"There's one approximately one hundred meters to your east."

"Copy."

"There's a building next to you, Jake. If you can cut through there, do it."

"Roger that."

Hawk moved along the asphalt at the rear of the large building until he found a stairway which led up to a landing halfway to the rooftop. "I think I've found a way in, Karl."

Starting his climb, he continued undetected to the top. Trying the door, it opened easily, so Hawk entered, noticing a long catwalk leading to the far end of the building.

Moving cautiously out across the metal walkway, doing his best to remain quiet, he could see through the green haze of his NVGs that whatever had been in the building had been removed. All that was left were empty crates and pallets.

"Bravo One, the target is still in play."

"Copy."

He reached the far end and tried the door blocking his progress. It too was open, and he cracked it wide enough to make his exit. On top of the landing, he looked down, noticing the guard opposite, standing post outside another building. This one smaller than the one he'd just traversed. There was no way he could get down there without the man seeing him.

Hawk raised the Bren2 and lined up the laser sight, stroking the trigger. No sooner had the guard hit the ground when he was down the stairs and dragging the body into the shadows. "X-Ray down."

Hawk frowned, his curiosity getting the better of him. "Alpha Two, are there any heat signatures coming from the building that X-Ray Two was guarding?"

"That's a negative, Bravo One."

The Brit eased himself around the front of the building, noting a set of large double doors. The Asphalt ran right up to them. Hawk grabbed one of the handles and pulled the door open far enough to squeeze through. Once inside he secured it behind him.

When he activated his flashlight and lifted his NVGs, he said, "Bingo."

"Say again, Bravo One," Ilse called over the comms.

"Ilse, love, I'm looking at a large stash of arms. Karl was right, this is where Medvedev keeps weapons. I'm going to have a look around."

"Don't take too long, Jake. Those guards will be missed eventually."

"I'll just be a jiffy."

In the minutes he was there, Hawk found automatic weapons, handguns, rocket launchers and ammunition. He took a further minute to leave a charge planted amongst it before swiftly exiting the building.

He pressed further into the complex and as he eased around the corner of another building, he found the last guard. Hawk let the Bren2 hang from its strap and slid his knife from its sheath. Using all his stealth, he crept towards the man, who remained blissfully unaware until it was too late. The Brit's hand clamped over his mouth as the knife drove into the side of his neck three times.

Once again, Hawk dragged him back into the shadows and lay him out of sight. He was about to continue his mission when the man's radio came to life.

"Oleg, are you there?"

Hawk stared at the radio.

"Oleg, report."

Hawk held his breath.

"Oleg, report!"

The Brit waited.

"Grisha, report."

Things were about to change. "Alpha One, Bravo One, I think I may be rumbled."

———

"SOMETHING IS WRONG," Varkov said to Rogov and Leonid. "I can't raise any of the guards."

"What about the towers?" asked Rogov.

"They are fine. No problem."

"Get everyone out. I want the complex searched from top to bottom."

"On it."

Rogov turned to Leonid. "You should get yourself and Viktor on the helicopter and leave."

"I was afraid something like this would happen," Leonid growled.

"Go, now. I'll take care of everything here."

"What if it's nothing?"

Rogov snorted derisively. "It is never nothing."

The Russian mercenary picked up his AK-12 and headed for the doorway leading into a larger room. As he traversed the length of it, Luba rose from an old sofa she'd found amongst the detritus of the complex. "What is going on, Kir?"

"Get your tight little ass up and moving," he growled at her. "We may have a problem."

She grabbed her body armor and slipped into it. As she did, she kicked Pavel in the ribs as he slept on the floor beside the sofa. "What is it? I'm busy screwing big tit Swedish girl."

"Put your dick away, Comrade. There is trouble afoot."

"She will be disappointed."

Luba picked up her AK-12. "Most likely relieved," she shot back at him.

"You are a cruel woman, Luba."

"Maybe when we are done here you can have me, Pavel."

He sighed as he shrugged into his own body armor. "And heartless as well."

As she left the room, Luba met Devin, the fifth of their

team. He was already kitted up and set to go. Except for one small detail. "Get your NVGs, dumbass."

"Shit."

"When you've got them, meet me outside."

By the time Devin emerged, Luba was already issuing orders to everyone that Varkov had dragged from their bunks. "Pavel, take three men and sweep the north part of the complex. I'll take three with me and do the south. Devin, the same with you. Go west. Fedor, take the remaining man and secure the helicopter. Go now."

———

"BRAVO ONE, Alpha Two. You were right, they're awake. You've got three groups of X-Rays starting to search the complex. One group moving towards—shit!"

"What?"

"It looks like there's a helicopter that we missed in the eastern part of the complex."

"Say again, Alpha Two."

"A helicopter on the eastern side."

Hawk felt his anger rise. "How could you not see a fucking helicopter?"

"It must've come in just before dark. Suggest you secure it quickly before anyone can use it to get away."

The Brit was sure he meant Medvedev. "Roger that."

"The quickest route will be through the center of the complex, Jake. But—"

"But what?"

"You've got X-Rays coming straight at you."

"Any way around, Alpha Two?"

"Not that I can see and have you make the helicopter in time," came the reply.

"Ever heard the expression, hold my beer, Karl?" Hawk asked.

"No, and I'm not sure I want to."

"Just sit back and watch."

Before he even moved, Hawk took the trigger from his pocket and set off the explosives he'd planted on the two light towers. They both went up with a roar as orange balls of flame rolled skyward. From there he put the suppressed Bren 2 up to his shoulder and started to press forward.

When he reached the end of the building, he turned right. The asphalt ran straight away from him towards another large warehouse. He hurried forward, his head on a swivel just in case. Then through the green haze four men appeared, running carelessly towards him.

The Bren2 fired as soon as his laser sights came on. A burst of fire and the runner he'd aimed at fell in an untidy heap, his weapon spilling from his grasp. Hawk stopped and fired another burst. The second shooter went down on his face and never moved.

The first of the remaining two to recover was a shooter who seemed to take the incoming fire in his stride. He dropped to a knee and opened up.

Hawk threw himself to the side as bullets cut through the air where he'd just been standing. An old 44-gallon drum appeared in front of the Brit, and he took shelter behind it. Rounds hammered into the metal exterior, and the empty vessel rang loudly under each impact.

"Fuck!" Hawk hissed and leaned out far enough to fire a long burst.

Small explosions erupted from around the other shooter who was trying to bring his weapon into play. Hawk adjusted his aim and fired the rest of his magazine, blowing the hapless shooter onto his back.

Hawk ducked back and dropped out the spent magazine while the shooter fired another long burst at the drum, hoping to flush his quarry from cover. However, the former SAS man was patient. He replaced the empty magazine, charged the Bren, and waited until the firing stopped.

This time instead of leaning out, he stood up, catching the shooter reloading. Hawk placed the laser sight on the man's chest and fired three rounds into his body armor. The target cried out, falling back, squirming under the pain of the impacts. Hawk walked toward the helpless man, reaching him and putting a bullet in his head.

"The gunfire has attracted some attention, Jake," Karl said. "You have more closing on your position."

"What's the status on the helicopter, Alpha Two?"

"If you can keep going you should get there about the same time as they do."

"Roger that."

―――

*Belarus Safehouse*

Grizz Harvey's eyes flickered across the screen. "There's a third team closing with the second. You need to tell him to go right."

"If he does that, he's going to miss the helicopter," Karl pointed out.

"And if he doesn't, he'll walk into a brick wall."

"Jake, copy?" Ilse asked.

"I'm still here."

"You've now got two teams, eight X-Rays, closing your position. If you go around, you'll miss the helo. Your call."

"I've got this," he replied.

They watched in silence as he stopped.

"What's he doing?" Ilse asked.

"Don't know," Karl replied.

"I do," Harvey said. "The stupid son of a bitch is crazy."

Hawk remained motionless for a couple more minutes and Ilse was worried. "Jake, they're almost on you. The others have all but reached the helicopter. What are you doing?"

There was a crackle of comms and a familiar voice said, "See you on the other side."

"Jake, no!"

———

WITH HURRIED MOVEMENTS, Hawk set the timers on the explosive bricks for thirty and forty seconds. He then threw them as far as he could. Almost immediately, the combined force appeared to his front, unaware of what was about to happen.

The first brick exploded violently, ripping into the attackers. Two fell instantly. The others scattered. When the second brick exploded, they were already in cover, but still the detonation disoriented them.

Hawk then stood and pulled the pin on a grenade. As he started forward, he threw it close to where an attacker was hiding. It detonated and the shooter was blown into the air.

He repeated his actions twice more. Looking like some Eighties' action hero, he brought the Bren2 up and began firing it.

Luba cursed vehemently as she saw the man coming towards them. She fired her weapon and saw him flinch, his left arm dropping from his weapon. But instead of trying to find shelter, the shooter surprised her as she watched through the haze of her NVGs, seeing him release the gun on its strap and take out a handgun.

Her jaw dropped when she realized that her demise was imminent. And as her brain registered the thought, it was suddenly gone as a bullet punched into her head.

Hawk saw the shooter fall and gave a satisfied grunt as pain burned through his left arm. The numbness was wearing off and feeling was starting to return. He walked purposefully forward past two squirming figures. One was dressed as the guards were. The other was better equipped and Hawk figured him to be part of Rogov's mercenary team.

The Brit shot them both in the head as he went by.

"How are we looking on that helicopter, Alpha One?"

"It's still on the ground, Jake. But I'd say it's spinning up."

Hawk started jogging. His arm throbbed but he pushed the pain from his mind. Rounding a corner, the helicopter was there, its main rotor just reaching takeoff speed.

"Jake, there's a vehicle leaving the complex to the north," Karl informed him.

"What the fuck do you want me to do about it?" he growled as the helicopter started lifting skyward in front of him.

Grinding his teeth against the pain, Hawk dropped the SIG and grabbed at the Bren2. He brought it level and fired what was left of the magazine at the aircraft. Bullets ricocheted off it everywhere and for a moment, Hawk thought it a waste of time. But suddenly the helicopter dipped to the left and crashed into the ground, its rotor shearing off and flying away. It was followed by the tail which snapped on impact as the helicopter rolled over and over before coming to a stop in the middle of a grassed area.

"That'll do it," Hawk grunted.

He approached the smoldering wreckage and noticed a crumpled form upon the ground. He leaned over it. The man was wearing a suit and was face down. Medvedev? "Alpha One, I've possibly got eyes on the HVT. I'm turning him over to find out."

Hawk reached down and grabbed the prone figure by the shoulder to turn him when gunfire erupted, and bullets cut through the air all around the former SAS man.

Hawk threw himself to the ground, rolling across the grass to get away from almost certain death. A bolt of pain rocketed through his arm making Hawk gasp for breath. He came up on one knee and felt for the Bren2. It wasn't there; he'd work out later that a bullet had come close enough to cut the strap holding the weapon. The Brit's hand dove for the holstered SIG.

In front of him, a bloody and battered Kir Rogov stood erect, his AK-12 rhythmically hammering its staccato tune. A bloody sneer was etched on the mercenary leader's face as he tried his best to kill the adversary before him.

Hawk steadied his aim and fired the SIG. The first round hit Rogov in the chest plate, stopping him cold. His second bullet hit the mercenary square in the forehead, snuffing out his life.

Hawk walked over to the prone figure he'd been forced to abandon when Rogov appeared. He reached down and turned the person over.

"Don't shoot! Don't shoot!" Hands leaped up in a defensive gesture.

One look at the bloodied face and Hawk could tell this was not Medvedev. With a snarl of anger he raised the SIG and pointed it at Leonid's head. "Wait," the desperate man pleaded. "I can help. I have information."

Hawk's finger tightened on the trigger.

"I know everything."

"Fuck," Hawk hissed and lowered the SIG. "Was he in the vehicle?"

"Yes."

"Where? Where did he go?"

"I don't know."

"Alpha One, this is Bravo One, over."

"Copy, Bravo One."

"Tell me you have eyes on the vehicle that left here."

"Negative, Jake."

"Well then, Alpha One. The Eagle has flown. Come and pick me up."

There was a moment's hesitation before the reply came through. "Roger, Bravo One. The bird will be onsite in two mikes. Good work."

"Yeah," Hawk muttered to himself. "Good work my ass."

# EPILOGUE

*Italy, Two Months Later*

"I HAVE eyes on the target building, Alpha One," Hawk said as he peered through the night vision binoculars. "I see three X-Rays, all armed."

"Copy, Bravo One. Bravo Two, sitrep?"

"I've got four X-Rays within my field of vision," Harvey replied.

"Karl, what do you see?"

The former German Intelligence officer tapped a few keys on the computer, his eyes never leaving the screen. "I confirm seven X-Rays around the perimeter."

"All right, we go in quietly. I want it confirmed that Helen Dorset is onsite before you go loud. Her parents in Canada have waited long enough for good news. Let's not stuff it up."

"Bravo One moving in for a closer look."

"Be careful, Jake."

The location for Helen Dorset had been revealed to them by Leonid. The man had almost been right when stating he knew everything. The one thing he didn't know was the location of Medvedev himself. However, they planned to use him anyway. This raid was just the start. If they kept pushing hard then maybe, one day, Medvedev would raise his head above ground once more.

Upon further investigation and questioning, it had been revealed that Helen was now the property of Alberto Rossi, Mafia boss, and prostitution king of the northern half of Italy. He'd had many dealings with Medusa who'd supplied him with many girls over the years. But every so often, he took a shine to a particular girl and kept her for his own pleasure until once more he became disenchanted and sent her away.

But for now...

Hawk slipped over the concrete parapet which bordered the front garden of the estate. He sank down and waited for the first of the guards to come to him. From where he was hidden amongst the shrubs, he could hear only the footsteps.

Karl's voice filled his ear. "Target, ten meters. Eight meters. Five meters...four...three...

Hawk came out of the garden foliage and clamped his hand over the guard's mouth. The knife rose and plunged three times before being drawn across the flesh of the throat.

The Brit lowered him into the garden out of sight before continuing his mission.

"Jake, hold, hold."

Hawk turned his head the instant he heard the footfall. One of the guards had moved from his position and stumbled across Hawk. The man opened his mouth to shout a warning when a bullet whistled out of the night and hit him in the head.

"X-Ray down," Nemo's voice was cool, calm.

Hawk pressed forward and moved around the side of the house. The MP5SD he carried up at his shoulder. He approached a mullioned window he knew to be unlocked.

He'd unlocked it earlier in the day while on a callout to the mansion to fix a faulty alarm system.

Hawk opened the window slightly, testing it. Nothing happened so he opened it the rest of the way and climbed in.

Dropping catlike to the floor, he paused and listened for movement. Nothing.

"Bravo One has reached Monty. Continuing mission."

"Copy, Bravo One."

Moving stealthily through the study until he reached the door leading out into the foyer, he opened it a crack and peered through the gap. It was clear. "Bravo One moving to Percival."

The Brit slipped out through the opening into the foyer. The slate-covered floor masked his passage as he walked towards the wide staircase. His boot had only just touched the first step when a man appeared in a doorway to his right.

Hawk spun and squeezed the trigger before anything could happen. The sound of empty casings falling on the hard floor echoed throughout the foyer. Hawk held his breath as the man fell, waiting to see if what had just happened would draw any unwanted attention.

When no one else emerged, he moved swiftly to drag the body beneath the stairs. Hawk climbed to the landing and walked along a wide hallway to a room where earlier in the day he'd been ordered to stay out of.

Hawk tried the door, but it was locked. "Alpha One, I've reached Percival. The door is locked. Am going loud."

"Jake—"

The Brit stepped back and kicked the door. Wood splintered and the door flew back, crashing against the wall. Through his NVGs he saw the covers fly back on the bed. A high-pitched scream filled the room as a young woman appeared. Hawk rushed forward, pinning her to the bed. "Are you Helen Dorset?"

The young woman struggled violently, and Hawk had to increase his pressure to hold her down. "Are you Helen Dorset?" he repeated a little louder.

This time his words broke through the curtain of fear. "Yes, yes I am."

"Stay there, I'm here to get you out. Alpha One, Jackpot, I say again, Jackpot. Send in the cavalry."

"Well done, Jake. Mister Harvey and his team are moving to your location."

"It's good to have you back, ma'am," Hawk said as he walked towards the doorway to ready himself for the coming assault.

At the other end, Anja smiled. "It's good to be back, Jake."

———

12 Hours Later

The locks on the steel door opened and the heavy metal structure swung back with a squeal of protest. Anja Meyer walked in through the opening and sat down opposite Leonid Fedorov, a stainless-steel table separating them. Leonid smiled and raised his chained hands. "Maybe?"

Anja gave him a tired smile. "Not in this lifetime."

The Russian shrugged. "It was worth a try."

"Your intelligence worked out. We took Rossi off the board and his brothels have all been shut down. We were able to cross off twenty women who were trafficked to his establishments."

"Is that all?" Leonid asked nonchalantly. Then he smiled. "I figured it would be at least double that. I suppose some is better than none at all. How are your wounds? You look to have recovered rather well."

Anja's left hand streaked across the table, grabbing the chains attached to his wrists and tugged them forward. As

Leonid lurched partially across the table, Anja's right hand, palm out. Smashed into the center of his face, flattening his nose. "You're a despicable human being," she hissed as blood splattered from the broken snout.

Leonid reeled back, blood streaming, tears rolling down his cheeks. "You bitch," he screeched. "You fucking bitch."

Anja stood up. "Have fun rotting in prison for the next two-hundred years, asshole."

"Wait," Leonid shouted after her.

Anja turned back. "What?"

"Hakim Anwar."

She stared at him. "What about him?"

"I can help you get him."

"How?"

"He bought some girls from Medusa. They were transported to Sudan."

"What for?"

"There is a terrorist training camp in the Nubian desert. They are short of women."

Anja felt her heart lurch. Sliding back down into the chair, she took out her cell and opened the recording app. Smiling at him, she said, "Tell me all you know."

# A LOOK AT BOOK TWO
## TALON JUSTICE

**The team that instils fear in its opponents...**

It all starts with a car chase in Antwerp, Belgium. As the Talon team tries to find the location of a terrorist camp in the Nubian desert to rescue a handful of girls sold to Mustafa Osman, they aren't expecting intel that points towards one of the captees being Polly White—the daughter of the British Home Secretary.

Sent in to secure the prisoners, Jacob Hawk finds that he's too late. Polly White has been relocated, and things aren't adding up. As team Talon's search for answers falls one step behind, lies and subterfuge abound. But once the truth is revealed...it's one stranger than fiction.

Will their war with Medusa get turned on its head?

*AVAILABLE NOW*

# ABOUT THE AUTHOR

A relative newcomer to the world of writing, Brent Towns self-published his first book, a western, in 2015. *Last Stand in Sanctuary* took him two years to write. His first hardcover book, a Black Horse Western, was published the following year.

Since then, he has written 26 western stories, including some in collaboration with British western author, Ben Bridges.

Also, he has written the novelization to the upcoming 2019 movie from One-Eyed Horse Productions, titled, *Bill Tilghman and the Outlaws*. Not bad for an Australian author, he thinks.

Brent Towns has also scripted three Commando Comics with another two to come.

He says, "The obvious next step for me was to venture into the world of men's action/adventure/thriller stories. Thus, Team Reaper was born."

A country town in Queensland, Australia, is where Brent lives with his wife and son.

In the past, he worked as a seaweed factory worker, a knife-hand in an abattoir, mowed lawns and tidied gardens, worked in caravan parks, and worked in the hire industry. And now, as well as writing books, Brent is a home tutor for his son doing distance education.

Brent's love of reading used to take over his life, now it's writing that does that; often sitting up until the small hours, bashing away at his tortured keyboard where he loses himself in the world of fiction.

Made in United States
Troutdale, OR
08/15/2023